Hello

By

K. L. Smith

Dedicated to my stalker

Prologue

Hello.

I'm so glad you've finally noticed me. I've been watching you for a while now - although trying to keep a respectful distance until I'm sure you're ready. Every night I watch your bedroom window from the street outside. Sometimes you tease me, leaving your lamp on longer than usual, are you trying to make me wait?

I keep myself cloaked from your view by the shrubbery in your neighbour's garden. It gets cold out here and sometimes I have to warm my hands on the light above your neighbour's gate; but I don't mind, you're worth it. I know you don't really know me yet, but you will, and one day you'll love me.

I started watching you a while ago. You were outside a shop looking like you were waiting for someone when you first caught my eye. There was just something about you, something…vulnerable. I breezed past you briefly and smelt the perfume in your hair. Coconut. Mm. I stood behind you, watching you. I think you must have known I was there as I saw the hairs on the back of your neck standing up as I reached a finger out to stroke your nape softly. I almost touched you before my nerve gave out and I retreated. I just had to know who you were, so I began following you.

I suppose you want to know my name?
Tough.

My name is of no consequence, I am love, I am desire, I am…hunger. We're meant to be together, you and I, and we will, I just know it.

I feel you, even when I can't see you. I dream of you, wake for you, and I'll die of you. You know me now, don't you? You must know who I am. Do you dream of me? I bet you do. You and I are meant to be together; we share a bond.

I know how you feel lost sometimes, alone and lonely even when you're surrounded by your friends. Life hasn't turned out quite as you thought it would has it? You never quite feel good enough. People tell you how good-looking you are, and you smile and say thank you, but you don't believe it do you? You aren't sure if they're just being nice, or even worse -sarcastic.

You fear you aren't doing your job very well, and one day someone's going to notice just how inadequate you are and fire you for it. And they will notice one day, but I'll be there to fix things for you.

I feel your loneliness and your pain, I'm here to help. Call me your guardian angel if you like. I'm going to make things all better, YOU JUST HAVE TO LET ME IN.

Yesterday before you left the house, I crept in through your back door while you were showering. I'm sure you must've left the door open for me on purpose as you seem to like to tease me. I hid under your bed while I waited for you to finish showering.

Did you drop your towel on purpose to torment me? You knew I was under there, didn't you? You knew I'd come in through that unlocked door. Well I wasn't going to bite…yet, I wasn't ready. You weren't ready either.

Once you'd gone I had a look around your home. I've been in your home lots of times before but I never snooped through your things before, I'm not a creep. However yesterday was different, you'd almost invited me to snoop, hadn't you?

I found the box of photos you never seemed to get around to putting into albums, I only took the ones I needed, I didn't recognise many people in the rest, but the ones I did recognise, I burnt. You know why.

Why doesn't the clock in your living room say the right time? I don't like that; it sets my teeth on edge. I fixed it for you. I'm sure you'll be pleased.

I hope you don't mind, but I took a coin from the pile of change near your washing machine, although it's not really stealing though is it, not when what's mine is yours and what's yours is mine.

Before I left I found your toothbrush by the sink, still damp from your own morning routine. I had to use it, it made me feel so close to you. I put it back as I found it though, you'd never know I borrowed it.

Chapter One

"That creepy man's watching you again," my friend Ruby observed from over her magazine.

I turned to see who she was looking at. I spotted a man wearing headphones who looked up as I turned around. He didn't look familiar though. I moved around a little in my seat and got a better view around the room. Oh, yeah now I knew who she meant. I gave an involuntary shudder. The man in question was about forty-something and painfully unattractive. His dark hair was pasted to his acne-ridden forehead with about a month's worth of grease. I could see he was staring at me over the top of a book he was pretending to read and as he caught my eye he looked away blushing.

"Not again!" I complained under my breath. "Is he following me or what?"

"Looks like it, this is the third time this week I've seen him watching you."

"Come on," I said, getting to my feet, let's just go back to work early. I'm suddenly not very hungry."

Ruby shook her head and sighed before sliding her magazine into her huge handbag and drinking the last of her cappuccino. "Wait up!" She called after me as I hurried for the exit.

Once we left the café I felt a little foolish, so what if a man was staring at me, I get that all the time. I really shouldn't let it bother me so.

"Hey Paula, look at that!" She suddenly called out making me jump.

"What?"

"Singles night!"

I followed her gaze to a sign that was hanging outside of our usual pub advertising a singles night that evening. I inwardly cringed as I knew what was coming next.

"We have to go!"

"Oh no, definitely not. You don't know what weirdos go to something like that."

"What, weirdos like us you mean?" She grinned, slipping her arm through mine. "Come on, it'll be fun. What do we have to lose?"

"Self-respect?" I suggested.

"How are you ever going to meet someone if you won't put yourself out there? Come on it's just one night out? What were your plans tonight anyway? Sit home alone and watch Netflix till you fall asleep?"

Okay, she may have a point. "Fine, I'll give it a go. But I'm only doing this for you, understood?"

"Understood." She grinned. "Now what the hell are we going to wear?"

***

I arrived home early for a change having beaten rush hour. I didn't know why I was so against being stuck in traffic, as it wasn't as if there was anyone at home waiting for me. What did it matter, being stuck in the driving seat or stuck to the sofa, either way I'd be bored and lonely.

I let myself in and dropped my keys into the bowl beside my front door, kicked my shoes off that were killing me and flipped the central heating thermostat to ON. I took my coat off and shivered my way into the kitchen to make a cup of coffee.

While I waited for the kettle to boil I decided to raid the change from above my washing machine so that I'd have money for the parking meter later on. I really ought to get a piggy-bank for my loose change, I'm just not that organised. Hell, I'm not even organised enough to empty my pockets before I load my washer - hence the huge pile of change that's always rattling around in the drum.

Strange, I thought, I could've sworn I had a pound-coin in amongst the copper and silver? Oh well, I must've dreamed it. I'd have to borrow change for the meter.

As I carried my cup through to the living room I noted my answer machine flashing in the dark. I put my cup down on the coffee table before walking over to the answer machine and pulling its cord from out of the socket. I wasn't in the mood for it tonight, it never brought me good news. One of these days I'll get around to throwing the damned thing away.

I settled down in front of the TV with my coffee and the book I'd been trying to finish for the past week, before giving up and putting the book down with a bang. I'd been really trying with this book but I just couldn't get into it. I couldn't focus enough. Normally I liked a good book in bed as it helped me fall asleep easier, lulling my brain away to the land of nod, but lately I just couldn't concentrate. Something about having my bedroom light on was unnerving me, it made me feel…vulnerable. Late at night my little bedside lamp felt like a beacon in the dark, a lighthouse of sorts guiding unwelcome things to my bedroom door.

I didn't like it.

Maybe Ruby was right, maybe I've been alone for so long that I've gone a little peculiar.

I don't like being alone though, I'm not on my own by choice. One things for certain, I can spot other lonely people like me a mile off. I think we must stink of desperation. God, how bad is that singles evening going to smell?

***

With my borrowed pound-coin I just managed to park in the last space in the carpark next to the pub. It was dark now and I felt a little unnerved as I made my way past all the dark cars, cringing at the loud echo of my steps. Turing around the corner I leapt out of my skin as Ruby pounced on me.

"Jesus Christ!" I gasped at her laughing face. "You scared the crap out of me!"

"Sorry, I just dashed out when I spotted your car pull in. Come on inside, I've got us a table."

I followed after her with butterflies flapping their way around my insides. How the hell had I got roped into this?

"Over here!" She called as she marched ahead to a small table next to the bar. "I've already got you a drink."

"Thanks." I said, taking a seat opposite her. I lifted the ridiculous cocktail umbrella out of the drink she'd ordered me and set it to one side before taking a long necessary drink.

"So what do you think?" She asked looking around her. "See anyone you like the look of?"

I wanted to throw my drink at her and make a run for the door, but instead I humoured her and took a cursory look around. As I expected, the place stunk to the high heavens of desperation. You could almost smell the latex from the condoms the men had brought 'just in case.' I had another longer look around before my eyes settled on a man who I'd seen around many times before. He stood out by the fact of how handsome he was compared to the other sad cases in here, he definitely didn't belong in a place like this and I never would've expected to find him here. He caught my eye for a moment before we both looked away quickly.

Ruby followed my departing gaze. "Oh, now I see why you're blushing. Mr dreamboat's here."

"What?" I flushed, "don't be stupid."

She shook her head smiling knowingly. "Every time we bump into him you start blushing and stammering. Now's your chance, go over and say hello."

"No." I was starting to panic at the thought of it. "I'm too shy. I'd die on the spot."

"He probably feels the same about you. Now go!" She dismissed me with a wave of her hands.

Before I knew what was happening my feet had started walking over towards him. What the hell was I thinking? I couldn't just go over there and start talking, what would I say? Oh my god I could barely even remember my own name!

Just as I was going towards him, the front door banged open startling me. I turned to see who had made such a loud entrance when I realised it was the creepy man from the café again. He locked eyes with me as he slowly walked across the floor towards the bar. I briefly smelt the acrid odour of sweat as he walked past me making my senses feel violated.

I turned on my heels and went and sat back down at my table.

"Chicken!" Ruby observed as I slinked into my seat.

"Better a live chicken than a dead one." I moaned.

Chapter Two

EXHIBIT B

When you passed by me in the bar I almost exploded with love for you, you looked RIGHT AT ME! Oh my sweet, how I adore you.

The time's getting nearer when we shall be together forever. You always look so sad; it breaks my heart to see how much your soul hurts. Nobody appreciates just how special you are, but I see it, I worship at its alter and pray to sip from its cup. You are mine, my beloved, my reason for living and my reason for dying. One day soon, my love.

***

Several times I tried to summon up the courage to go talk to Mr Dreamboat, but I just couldn't do it.

"Wimp!" Ruby observed when she came back to our table. "Do you see that blonde guy over there with the red T-shirt on? He just gave me his number. We're going to go out over the weekend. If you'd have bothered to ask Mr Dreamboat out, we could've double-dated."

I really wasn't enjoying the evening one bit. "This just isn't for me, Ruby. I'm glad it's worked out for you, but it really isn't my scene."

"You haven't even *tried* though Paula." She spun me around and pushed me in the back. "Go, talk to him, now!"

I found myself hurtling towards Mr Dreamboat at a speed that made me feel most uncomfortable. He looked equally uncomfortable, and turned and walked away, leaving me hanging like some kind of moron. I watched in disbelief as he put his coat on and headed out of the door without a backwards glance.

I shuffled over to Ruby, shamefaced and muttered, "I'm going home."

"Oh don't be silly, there's plenty more fish in the sea. Over there for example. She added with a giggle."

I turned to see the creep from the café staring at me. Ugh. I turned back to her and slid my coat on. "I repeat, I'm going home." I picked my keys up and bid her goodnight.

"Don't drink and drive." Ruby called after me as I headed for the door.

"I won't." I called back, and put my car keys in my pocket.

***

Once I was home I could remove my brave-face and leave it on the nightstand until I needed it in the morning. I climbed into bed, unmasked, lonely and unloved.

I picked up my book and attempted to settle into it again. I seriously needed the distraction. There's nothing like rejection to make you feel small and lost is there? I hate to admit this to myself, but I need saving. I can't do it myself. I need someone to sweep in and pick me up and save me.

I was disgusted with myself for having such archaic thoughts. "So much for being a feminist!" I chided my reflection as I caught its judgemental eye across the room. She shook her head at me looking disappointed.

Once more I settled down to my book, but after a few pages in I became very aware of the crack in my bedroom curtains. It was only small, but it was definitely there. I tried to ignore it and turned back to my book. Despite my best efforts my eyes kept returning to the crack in the drapes.

That wouldn't do. That wouldn't do at all.

I felt with my hand along the side of my bed until I felt my dressing gown. Despite always sleeping naked, now I suddenly felt very protective of my bare skin. I slid the robe on under my quilt before getting out of bed and reaching out tentatively to pull the curtains shut a little tighter.

I had a bad feeling.

I stood there staring at my closed drapes for a moment wondering what I would see if I flung them open wide. Would I see nothing but darkness broken up slightly by the light above my neighbour's gate? Or would there be someone on the other side of the glass staring in at me? My hand hovered around the fold in the fabric while my heart pounded out its own special rhythm in my chest. I folded as my nerve dropped and I ran across the room and slid under my bedclothes before pulling the quilt over my head.

As the panic in my veins subsided a little I felt foolish. What was wrong with me lately? Why were my nerves so frazzled? The hair on the back of my neck seemed to be creeping up at the strangest moments and my nerves seemed to be on red alert.

I suddenly got a wave of panic as I thought about the light still burning away next to my bed. If there was someone outside, they might not be able to see me, but they could see my silhouette, couldn't they?

I cautiously slid the quilt down and looked around my room. Yes, my shadow could be clearly seen against the curtains. I reached a handout and fumbled for the switch, plunging myself into darkness.

I don't know what was worse, being seen in the light, or unable to see something coming in the dark. I decided to get up and get dressed as it was safer.

***

Once I was up and dressed I felt a little better. I pondered my strange state of mind as I waited for the kettle to boil. I wasn't a nervous person normally, but something was clearly wrong with me. My Spidey senses were working overtime at the moment for some reason. Perhaps I was cracking up? Maybe this is what happens when you get lonely? Your brain starts playing tricks on you. Shit, I really need a man. It was a shame Mr Dreamboat had scarpered. I could use his company tonight.

Chapter Three

EXHIBIT C

When you left early I was disappointed, but it created an opportunity that I had been pondering all day. When I was in your house, I opened the catch on your kitchen window. I left the window in the closed position, but would you notice the catch wasn't on?

While you paced up and down outside of the pub waiting for a taxi, I got in my car to try and beat you home. I wanted to know; did you leave the window open for me? Did you notice what I did? Did you notice but leave it open for me anyway?

***

As I pulled up outside your house I realised I'd beat you home. Yay!

I parked my car around the corner out of sight and made my way back to your house. The wave of excitement fluttering through my heart as I opened your gate and crept up the dark path towards your back door was indescribable! I approached the kitchen window with anticipation, would it be open? Would I be barred from your house, your life, your bed?

Or would I be invited?

I felt around the window frame but my fingers couldn't find purchase. After a moment I pulled my car key out and slid it under the frame. My breath caught in my throat as I felt the frame move. Oh the feeling of euphoria as the window swung open was indescribable!

I pulled the window open as far as it would allow and carefully climbed inside, landing gracefully on the other side without knocking anything over - to my great relief. Feeling delighted with myself, I pulled the window closed behind me and slid the catch down tight.

Now for somewhere to hide till I decide the time is right.

***

I was surprised how late it was when I looked at the clock. Either I was out a lot longer than I thought, or I had fallen asleep for a while after reading my book. 4am the clock yawned at me, as I settled on the couch with my book, again. At least I felt more safe in my living room, particularly as I was now fully dressed. I don't know why I'd been so unnerved earlier. I suppose it's that eerie feeling of being watched or something.

I lay out on the couch with the TV on mute while I began my book for the third time that evening. I know there was no real reason for the TV to be on, but it made me feel less alone.

After half an hour I put the book down with a sigh. I just couldn't settle. Something still felt really…off. The house was so quiet – the silence was deafening. Maybe music would help? A house full of music never felt empty. But, what about the neighbours? It was a little late for music, wasn't it? Then again, I saw someone wearing headphones earlier, and that reminded me about my own headphones I had hidden away under my bed. Yeah, maybe that would make me feel better, nice bit of music, a bit more of my book and fall asleep on the couch.

I got up and slowly made my way out of my cosy living room and headed back up the stairs to my bedroom. The darkness of the stairs and landing was unsettling me a little again. I flicked the switch to turn the landing light on but the bulb must've gone. With a groan, I flicked it a couple of times just to make sure, but nothing. I sighed and continued my ascent.

As I made my way across my bedroom towards the bed I noted the gap in the top of the curtains was back. Didn't I re-close them? I pulled them firmly closed again, before turning towards my bed.

I couldn't see the junk that I knew was under there from here as I had a long valence sheet hiding my clutter from view. I got down on my hands and knees before reaching my arm under and feeling about through the various bits and pieces. I tilted my head to one side as I slid my arm further under the bed, before pulling it back in shock at the strange-warm thing I felt under there. "What the hell was that?" I gasped in panic, rubbing my arm.

I sat for a moment panting and wondering what to do?

I decided to be brave. This was my house and I refused to be terrorised. I grabbed the valence sheet decisively and pulled it up over my head giving me a clear view of what was under my bed.

"How dare you hide under there!" I yelled, as next-door's cat came charging out with a yelp, scratching me in the process. "Bloody CAT!" I bellowed as I chased it down the stairs and out of the front door. "Scared the crap out of me!" I chuntered out into the dark night to no one.

I retraced my steps, grabbed my headphones from under the bed and settled back on the couch with my book. I turned the volume up loud. Now nothing could bother me or disturb me.

***

EXHIBIT D

I slid out from under your spare bed once I knew you had your headphones on. I could walk about quite happily now as long as I kept out of your eyeline. I expected to tell you tonight how I feel, hell, show you how I feel… live for you, bleed for you, die for you… But I'm a coward. I don't think now is the right time after all.

I watched you for a while from the open door, you couldn't see me from your angle, but I could see you. You are so beautiful; you just don't know…

I noticed your answer machine was unplugged. Why? Didn't you want to hear my voice? I bent over and plugged it back into the wall. I turned back to look at you one last time. You make my heart hurt every time I look at you.

I had to leave you for a while, you hurt me too much. I decided to go lay in your bed for a while before I departed for the evening.

As I lay my head down upon your pillow I could smell your hair, coconut again. Heavenly. But this was dangerous, I could fall asleep here so easily. It's so comforting being this near to you…

***

I pulled my headphones off, puzzled. What was that? I'm sure I heard a bang. I stood up and cocked my head to one side listening. Was it the front door?

I made my way down the hall cautiously. I peered in every room as I passed, but nothing looked out of place. I was puzzled what the bang could've been. After ascertaining that nothing was wrong anywhere I took a bold step and opened my front door.

"Hello?" I called out to the darkness. "Is there anyone there?"

I leapt out of my skin as the annoying cat from next door shot out of my – now knocked-over dustbin.

"Shoo!" I shouted after it as it ran off into the night. I stood for a moment, peering after it into the darkness, seeing nothing but my own ghostly shrubbery. Finally, my gaze drifted across the road - where I could clearly see -skulking beneath my neighbour's gate-light –the creep from the coffee shop staring across at me.

I shot back in through the door and slammed it behind me. I locked the door as fast as my shaking hands would allow and then slid the security chain across. I stood with my back to the door, panting when I noticed my answer-machine was blinking in the darkness.

I had a message.

I ran down the hall and pulled the plug out of the wall with both hands. Had I plugged it back in? I couldn't remember. Regardless, that machine had a message that I didn't want to hear.

I stared over my shoulder at the front door. I really need better security. If he charged the door, would those locks hold?

Chapter Four

"So, last night was a waste of time then." Ruby sulked into her cappuccino.

We were back in the coffee shop during our lunch hour, though thankfully my night-time stalker wasn't here today. I'd been in two minds whether to mention my night visitor to Ruby or not before deciding against it. Ruby was a work colleague not a proper friend. There were things that she didn't know about me, and I wasn't sure I'd be comfortable explaining certain things just yet.

"Are you even listening?" She chastised, breaking me from my daydreaming.

"Sorry, what did you say?"

"What's up with you today? You've barely spoken a word all day."

"Oh, sorry. I didn't get much sleep last night."

"I wish I had a reason to be up all night last night. Mr Dreamboat could certainly keep me up all night if you know what I'm saying!" She laughed.

I bristled. "I saw him first."

She held up her hands submissively. "Hey, I'm only winding you up. I know he's out of bounds. But seriously, you *have* to ask him out sooner or later, you can't keep playing the shy card. Men don't like that. Men like an *assertive* woman, like me." She grinned.

I smiled weakly back at her and prayed for her to change the subject. I wasn't in the mood to dissect my pathetic love life, or rather, lack of one.

"So, what was your last boyfriend like?" She asked to my dismay.

I panicked for a moment. What could I tell her? I had a feeling she'd just keep digging till she wheedled it out of my me, she was just that sort of person.

Nosey.

I took a deep breath and reluctantly told her the truth. "He was amazing, but…he died."

I took a long drink of my coffee while she digested this piece of gossip. I knew it would be all around the office block by the end of the day, so I was careful to keep details to a minimum.

"Oh my god, that's awful! I had no idea!" She sat back in her seat for a moment staring at me open-mouthed. "Do you mind me asking, how did he die?"

"I'd really rather not talk about it if you don't mind, I'm trying my hardest not to think about it."

"I completely understand. Oh my god, I can't believe it. No wonder you're so strange about dating. You're still in love with him, aren't you?"

"Yes, I suppose that's it." I lied.

"Well don't you worry," she said, "your secret's safe with me. I won't tell anyone."

"Thanks, I'd appreciate that if you don't mind."

"It goes without saying. Cross my heart and hope to d…" She looked sheepish. "Anyway, we best be getting back hadn't we. Don't want to be late." She gave me a pained smile and hurried off.

I gathered my things together and left a tip on the table for the waitress before hurrying off after her. "Ruby, wait up!" I called, as she hurried on ahead. I'd obviously embarrassed her with my revelation. People are strange around you after someone dies. You get some people who fawn over you, desperate to appear sympathetic and sincere, and then there is the other type of people, those who cross the road to avoid you because they don't know what to say. To be honest I prefer the latter people.

***

By the end of the day it was obvious that word had spread around the office about my lost love. I could tell by the way the office had split into the two camps. One side were being desperately nice to me, and the other side were much more ignorant than usual.

I sidled up to Ruby as she made her way to the copy machine. "Did you tell everyone?"

She looked up sheepish. "Kind of. But I didn't mean to, it just sort of…slipped out."

"So much for keeping a secret," I fumed.

"I really didn't mean…."

We were suddenly aware of a commotion going on behind us. We turned to see what had people staring at our colleague John's computer screen with such fascination. As I approached the crowd gathered around the monitor my stomach dropped. John had obviously googled me – something that I hoped would never happen.

"This is you?" John asked me looking shocked.

I couldn't take my eyes off the computer screen as I saw my shocked face staring back at me from the front page of the newspaper that was uploaded in front of me. I stared at the headline that had been dancing around my brain for the last year: - INQUEST VERDICT – SELF DEFFENCE. MURDER CHARGES DROPPED.

I looked away feeling sick at the barrage of unwelcome memories that were flooding into my brain. I thought I'd managed to escape from my past by running away and starting a fresh somewhere new. I looked up to find Ruby looking closer at the monitor in front of us. After a moment, she snatched the mouse from John's sweaty hand and clicked the screen off before shooing everyone away.

"Alright," she bellowed, "show's over, piss off back to work will you?"

I was staring shame-faced at my feet when she put a kind hand on my shoulder and led me off to the break room.

I sank into the saggy armchair in the corner while she put the kettle on, staring at my hands that were gripping the chair arms for all I was worth. Now Ruby was going to want me to tell her all about it, wasn't she? What on earth could I say? How could I even form the words to explain?

"So…." She began as she put a cup down next to me before taking a seat on the small stool usually used for propping the door open. Today the door was firmly shut; probably with a few ears pressed up against it on the other side I shouldn't wonder. "Do you want to talk about it?" She asked.

"No, but I don't suppose I have a choice now do I? If I don't tell you, you'll just go back in there and read all the gory details for yourself."

She looked uncomfortable. "I'm really sorry, I didn't mean to blurt it out to them, it's just that John kept pressing me about if you met anyone at the singles night last night, and if I thought he'd have a chance if he asked you out. I said he had no chance because you're pining for a lost love, and he said, 'what did he die or something?' One look at my face and he guessed it and started googling you.

Look, I'm so sorry, I really didn't mean to hurt you."

I looked up at her contrite face and wanted to slap her. She'd just single handidly ruined everything for me. Now people would be gossiping about me behind my back, whispering, wondering, was it self-defence or was I a murderer? The truth was, I loved that man more than life itself, but when he tried to stab me for a second-time, self-preservation kicked in. The jury didn't know this, but I cried as I drove the knife into his heart. As I watched the life ebb from his beautiful eyes I felt my own heart die there right along with his on the linoleum of our kitchen floor. As he slumped to the floor I cried against his still chest and with my shaking finger, I drew a heart on the floor from our blood.

As I heard the sirens getting closer, the heart vanished in the flood of red that we bled.

"So?" Ruby urged me with a curious face that I didn't care for. "What happened?"

I flicked my annoyed eyes to hers. After a long pause, I answered her truthfully. "What always happens, love hurts."

***

EXHIBIT E

You seem so sad today? What's wrong my love? Soon. Soon we'll be together and then I can make you happy, no more of this moping around suffering at the hands of fools who should know better. I know you have suffered injustice and heartbreak; I am your happy-ever-after, you just don't know it yet…

It was dark when I arrived home with a stinking headache after a truly awful day. I had managed to dodge Ruby's questions for the remainder of the day but no doubt the barrage of questions will start again tomorrow. Probably all my work colleagues were googling me right this very minute. In all likelihood, I'd have to start looking for another job before the situation got out of hand. Before I was cleared of the murder charge I'd been the subject of endless abuse from both the tabloids and my local community. I received death threats almost on a daily basis from people who didn't know me from Adam, and certainly didn't know anything about my circumstances. I'd naively assumed that once I was cleared of all charges I'd be able to get back on with my life, but no, people just weren't built to be kind, it's their instinct to put something down that's wounded. I certainly wore the scars from their attempts, figuratively and physically. I rubbed my forearm self-consciously where I had been burned when I was forced down onto a lit barbecue one night as I tried to escape the mob that had surrounded my house. I passed the scar off as a birthmark when questioned on its origin. But it and I knew the truth.

I leaned down and turned the knob on the side of the fireplace igniting the gas and bringing my fire to life with its comforting warmth. The cold November weather was starting to seep into my bones every time I stepped foot outside. I kicked my shoes off and pulled my wet tights away from my soggy toes before sitting in front of the fire with my knees pulled up to my chest and my cold toes waiting on the fender for the warmth they craved.

I could feel that heavy weight of sorrow deep in my chest, and it would've been easy to cry, my eyes were threatening to rain down any moment, but I was determined to stay the cries. Enough tears had been shed to last me a lifetime. It just didn't get you anywhere did it? I know people say it's a stress relief, but I'm not sure anymore, sometimes I think that's an excuse people make up who don't have the guts to tell me to pull myself together and stop being a baby.

I contemplated my sorrowful existence as my frozen bones began to thaw, and as my body defrosted, so did my mood. This time, I decided, things were going to be different. No running away from everything anymore. After all, ignorance was the cause of my misery last time, people didn't know the facts and so they made them up and perpetuated rumours. This time I would make people know the truth. If they knew all of the gory details they wouldn't have to make them up would they? It would be hard, I knew, and for a while people would talk about me behind my back, but hopefully once they got bored of my story they'd drift off back to ignoring me again and I could carry on life as normal as possible. It was either that or move again and maybe change my name by deed pole. But why should I lose my identity, hadn't I lost enough?

***

After I had made myself a hot meal and had a soak in the bath I decided to do something proactive. If my work colleagues were googling me, it would help to know what was being said about me online, at least then I would know what rumours to quash. There was a tiny part of me hoping that there would be nothing online but the newspaper article exonerating me that I had seen earlier, but no. My heart sank as I saw the amount of forums listed as having entries with my name heading their posts. This was much worse than I thought. There were entire pages dedicated to me, some demonizing me, some glorifying me. It seemed pretty fifty/fifty – heroine/villain. I was a figurehead to abused woman for standing up to – and taking down my abuser, and an evil murderer - who got off on a technicality, to others. I found my mouse hovering over the entry with the most hits, I don't know if I clicked it on purpose or whether it was an involuntary gesture. I took a sharp intake of air as the page loaded up and I saw the images of my face taken on the day the mob surrounded me and whipped me with the chain of a dog lead before I managed to escape. I hadn't realised someone had been snapping away with a camera at the time. With a sinking feeling in the pit of my stomach I pulled the page down to get rid of the image and read the text below it. It seemed like a conversation between two people who were there.

Baz123: Murdering bitch got her just deserts!
Tony82: Told you we'd get that bitch good style. She won't know what's hit her when I'm done.

Baz123: Thinks she can just swan around here where our kids play does she? I don't fucking think so. That scumbags got to GO!

Tony82: I'm gonna burn her fucking house down while she sleeps lol.

That was as far as I got before I had to run to the bathroom to be sick. I could read no more. God only knew what my co-workers would think. I suppose tomorrow would tell?

Chapter Five

The following morning was better than I expected. To my surprise people were pretty much ignoring me as usual, no sly glances that I was aware of - though Ruby's sympathetic looks were getting on my nerves a bit, but hell, all things considered, I could cope with that. The only real mention of anything came from John -he who was responsible for googling me. He popped over to see me briefly and apologised for 'outing me.'

"I'm so sorry," he said again, "it's obvious you've had a hell of a time and been through the wringer, but, you're with friends here. We're all here to support you."

I struggled to hide my surprise. "Thanks, it just came as a shock to see that article on your computer."

He looked contrite. "I'm really very sorry, I had no idea that would happen when I googled you."

He ended our little conversation by asking me out, so I don't suppose he believes me to be a cold-bloodied killer after all. I said no though, I'm just not looking to start anything new. My heart is still full of just one person -who won't leave it no matter how he hurts me and no matter how much I wish he'd leave me. I might be flawed as a person, but my heart is faithful to a fault – perhaps to my detriment.

"So," said Ruby sinking down next to me, "did he ask you out?"

"He did." I replied without looking up from my spread sheet.

"What did you say?"

"I said no."

She moaned loudly. "Why not? He's not bad looking that John, his hands are a bit soft and his hair's a bit floppy for me but nobody's perfect, well, except Mr Dreamboat maybe."

I turned to face her so she could clearly see the scorn upon my face.

"Okay, okay," she said backing off with her hands raised. "I get it, he's not your type."

"It's not that," I began, "it's just that there's been no one since…"

"David." She finished for me.

I didn't like his name on her lips, it felt wrong.

"Yes." I replied.

She stared at me for a moment. "Okay, I get it, you don't want to talk about what happened. It's completely understandable after what you went through. I won't keep going on about it, I promise."

I sighed and turned back to her. "Come around to mine tonight and I'll tell you all about it, but bring plenty of wine, I'm gonna need it to get through it!"

"Deal!" She whispered excitedly as she departed for her own desk.

***

Ruby was bang on time I noted as the knock on the door came at 7pm sharp. I took a deep cleansing breath and opened the front door.

"Hi," she said, as she strode past me and off into my living room.

"Make yourself at home." I whispered down-wind of her departing shadow. I shut the door and followed after her. I could tell by the sound of clinking bottles that she'd been true to her words and brought the Dutch courage I desperately needed.

"I've almost brought a rainbow," she beamed shrugging out of her overcoat. "Red, white and pink. Which do you prefer?"

"Red. I'll fetch the glasses."

"And a corkscrew!" She called after me.

I took a moment to collect myself as I gathered up the glasses and corkscrew. I wasn't entirely sure how much I was going to tell her, or even how I was going to start. The only explanation I have ever given was in court, and I was so traumatised that I don't actually have any recollection of giving my testimony. Stress induced amnesia I guess Oprah would say. Just in shock from what happened, I would say.

I handed Ruby the corkscrew and watched as her capable hands released the courage I would need from the bottle of merlot.

"Here," she said offering me the first glass.

"Thanks," I said meekly. I swirled the blood-like liquid in my glass thoughtfully for a moment before making my mind up and swallowing it down in one go. "Another please?"

She gave a slow smile as she took my glass and refilled it. "There you go."

I took it from her hands and this time set it down on the table in front of me as I sank into the sofa curling my legs up under me. I watched quietly as Ruby uncorked the bottle of chardonnay and poured herself a glass before taking a seat across from me. Once she was seated comfortably she raised her glass to me. "Cheers." She took a long drink from her glass -though I didn't join her. My glass remained on the table where I left it.

I felt my heart start to beat faster as she looked at me. She was waiting for me to begin.

I cleared my throat a little, and began. "He was called David, and I loved him, very much. Despite how he was at the end, he was the love of my life." I paused as I tried to collect my train of thought. "We met at work where we both worked in telesales for a glazing company. We'd both just left college and jobs were thin on the ground. It was a horrible job, getting shouted at and abused by people down the phone almost constantly, but David used to cheer me up and make me laugh, he could always make me laugh, no matter how down I was, and it wasn't long before we started dating. I think we both knew right away that we had something really special, we just…. fit. Do you know what I mean?"

Ruby nodded.

"I never believed in soul mates and all that romantic stuff till I met him, but he was…he was just so…so…amazing. We became inseparable. Within a month he asked me to move in with him, which I did without a second thought. The first six months were absolute heaven, I never knew that it was possible to love someone that much, suddenly all those dumb romantic songs made sense. It physically hurt to be apart from him. I don't think many people get to experience that kind of intense love, we felt so lucky to have what we had. Everything was…perfect." I stared down at my fidgeting hands. "Anyway, fast forward six months and the cracks were beginning to appear. He started getting really jealous and possessive. He didn't like it if I was out of his sight for any reason -to the point where I couldn't even go to work as we worked in different buildings after I got a promotion. I had to quit and stay home. Although he didn't like that either as he thought I was off galivanting every day, or worse inviting people around when he wasn't there. That was the point where he started locking me in every day while he was at work. Next he started cutting people out of our lives whom he deemed 'out to split us up.' It just got worse and worse and no matter how much I tried to make him happy and secure, his jealous behaviour just escalated exponentially. Soon he was turning out my pockets looking for receipts to check if I was lying about having to pop out to the shops for something. I was miserable and had no idea what to do. He'd never hurt me, I wasn't like some little battered wife, he'd never laid a finger on me. But I couldn't understand his cruelty, I loved him so much and never ever would have left him or cheated on him, no one could've driven a wedge between us, I was unequivocally his. So I was baffled as to what to do, leaving him was out of the question, I couldn't live without him. All I could do was try and ride it out and hope that eventually he would realise that his insecurities were for nothing and we could get back to normal. As long as I kept him happy he was the most wonderful loving person, but I knew there was something really wrong with him. He'd had a bad upbringing and spent a lot of time in care, so I just thought he needed to feel secure and wanted, but was just going about it all wrong. I was hoping to gradually acclimatise him to a normal relationship. Make him feel loved, wanted and secure and all the nonsense would stop." I paused for a moment to gather my composure. "This went on for months, getting worse and worse until one day he decided during a furious rage that the best thing for both of us would be if we were dead, then nobody could tear us apart, or so he said."

"So what did he do?" Ruby asked, on the edge of her seat, wine untouched.

"The long and short of it was…he stabbed me. When he went to finish the job and stab me a second time I grabbed a knife off the countertop and stabbed him. I didn't mean to kill him, I was aiming for the arm holding the knife, but I missed when he lunged suddenly and I caught him through the heart. He died in my arms." I fell into my memories for a few moments before continuing. "It wasn't long before I heard the sirens coming. My neighbours had heard my screams and had called the police.

"Wow!" Ruby exclaimed. "You've really been through it haven't you!"

"Just a tad, yes."

"I can't believe I didn't know this! I mean, we've been friends for six months and I didn't have a clue."

I took a grateful sip from my glass. "Where I lived before, people weren't very kind. Not everyone believed what had happened to me. David was a really popular man and everyone liked him, whereas not many people knew me, it was easier for them to think that their friend had been cut down by some ruthless killer than to believe that he was so screwed up he was willing to kill us both."

"Wow." She stared at me thoughtfully. "Have you considered selling your story? I bet you could make a bomb."

"Definitely not! Let's just say that my experience with the tabloids wasn't pleasant."

"Oh, okay." She fell silent for a while digesting the information I had just bombarded her with. "What did he look like? I bet he was good looking, right?"

I don't know if it was the wine making me more brave than usual but I did something that surprised us both. "I'll show you." I said as I got up and padded across the room and opened the box in the corner that still hadn't found a home for. With shaking hands I pulled away the loose photos off the top and pulled out a little black photo album edged in silver from underneath, passing it over to Ruby without looking at it.

She almost grabbed the thing off me with anticipation and pulled her feet up under her getting more comfortable to view my pain. I sat back down and finished off my wine before reaching across for the bottle and giving myself a top-up.

"I see what you mean," she said. "He was a hotty. In fact, he looks the spitting image of Mr Dreamboat. You certainly have a type."

"He does not! He doesn't look anything like him."

"Maybe just the same hair cut I suppose."

"Yeah, he grew it longer after that photo was taken." I said as she turned the photo around to show me. I wish she hadn't. The photo was taken in happier times and the memories were still too painful for me to view objectively.

"What happened to the other photos in the album?" She asked as she flicked through the rest of the book.

"I don't know, why?" I asked standing up and going over to see. As she turned the album to face me I saw where it looked like photos had been torn from the book. Four little corners on each page were all that were left as evidence that the book had ever been full. "I don't know." I said puzzled, turning the pages as I took the book from her.

"I noticed there's only the pictures of him left in there. Is it the photos of you that's been torn out?"

I nodded feeling my heart sink. I snapped the book shut. "Let's change the subject now. It's been a difficult thing to talk about. How about some more wine?" I picked the bottle of chardonnay up and began to fill Ruby's glass.

"Okay, no problem. Before I'm going to have any more wine though I'm going to have to lose some. Where's your toilet?"

"Up the stairs on the left."

"Great."

She was gone for quite a while to my relief, which gave me chance to try and think of something to change the subject. I'm not that great at chit-chat and usually rely on Ruby to steer the conversation, but tonight I didn't want her at the helm. She'd mentioned she was going on holiday soon so I was going to quiz her about that for a bit to get her onto a different topic. By the time she entered my lounge I was primed and ready.

"Hey Paula?"

"Mm?"

"Did you say there's not been any other men since 'you know who?'"

"Yes, I told you."

"Huh." She looked puzzled.

"What's wrong?"

"Nothing, it's just that there's a pair of men's cufflinks on your bathroom sink."

I felt myself pale a little. "Cufflinks? On my sink?"

"Yeah, a pair of silver ones. I suppose they're your dad's or something?"

I haven't seen my dad since I was thirteen.

"What's up Paula? You look odd. Didn't you know they were there or something?"

"No, I didn't."

She was looking funny at me. "It looks like someone took them off to roll their sleeves up while they washed their hands or something. Have you had a man around here lately? Plumber? Electrician?"

"A tradesman who wears cufflinks?"

She shook her head. "Yeah, strange that. Oh well I suppose there must be a simple explanation for it."

"Yeah." Though I couldn't think of a single reason.

She lifted her wine glass to mine and clinked them together. "Anyway, cheers."

Chapter Six

EXHIBIT F

My love for you is making me sloppy. I'm going to get caught, I just know it. But maybe that's how I want it. They say there's no such thing as accidents don't they?

I sometimes feel like a ghost that haunts you from afar, I'm in your life but only in the ethereal fringes. You probably know my face as well as a friend's yet you look through me as if I'm not there. I feel the imprint of your cold stare against my lips, caressing them with your contempt. Oh how you're going to love me soon, the time is so near for us my love.

Leaving cufflinks on the sink was a foolish oversight on my part, by the time I remembered they were there it was too late. I should have known they would raise unwelcome questions; my memory can be so foolish at times; I tend to leave things in the oddest places lately without being aware of it.

It's your fault, you distract me.

I may haunt your life, but you haunt my brain. You are the ghost in my machine, and I offer myself up freely for your possession.

***

Once Ruby had gone I picked up the cufflinks off the bathroom sink and turned them over in my fingers. They looked pretty old, possibly antique. I looked up and saw my pained face in the mirror over the sink as I handled them. Gosh I look frightened to death.

I looked about me for a moment before my eyes settled on the small cupboard below my sink. After one last look as my dark scared eyes I pushed the offending cufflinks to the back of the dark space.

**

It took me a while to fall asleep, all I could think about was David and our last day together. I've driven myself half-mad trying to think of anything I could've done differently that day. Something that would have saved him, saved us both. Eventually I did fall asleep, but I fell into the land of nightmares.

I think it was around three o'clock when I awoke to a loud crash outside. I leapt out of my skin and fumbled around in the dark trying to find a light switch. Finally, my hand found purchase and the light chased the dark from the room. Thankfully I spotted my dressing-gown where I'd left it on my dressing table stool. I gratefully covered my vulnerable nakedness and pulled the cord tight around my waist. Approaching the door fearfully, I stopped with my hand rested on the door handle. Did I really want to go out there? Did I really want to come face to face with what made that noise? Before I had chance to think, there came another crash, this time it sounded like a window breaking. Shit, someone was breaking in!

I picked up my mobile phone to dial the police but to my horror the battery was completely dead. "What do I do?" I whispered to myself as I dropped the useless phone onto my bed. The crashing about downstairs was escalating, this was no cat burglar, this was someone who didn't care if they woke me up. Oh god, was this personal?

I was shaking as I slid down the door with my back braced against it to try and stop someone entering. I was just wedging my toes up against the bedframe when things downstairs changed. I heard two distinct male voices, and they were shouting at each other. My ears pricked up as I heard my name mentioned during the scuffle that was taking place downstairs. I couldn't tell what was being said apart from that my name had been called out. I put my ear to the door to try and work out what was going on. Had someone disturbed the burglar?

I heard a lot more crashing as things downstairs were getting knocked over during the very obvious fight that was taking place. Eventually the crashing noise made it past the threshold of my front door. I crossed the room quickly to peek through my curtains and what was happening below. I could see the dark figure of someone holding another man around the throat before he launched him across the road with considerable strength despite his small stature. The man across the road picked himself up slowly and shouted, "She's dead. If she don't run, she's dead mate!" He then slowly hobbled off up the street chuntering to himself until his voice was a distant whisper on the wind.

I looked down to see the figure below stepping back into my house for a moment before I heard my door lock below me. The figure then slowly slipped away into the darkness across the street.

It took me a long time before I could find the courage to creep downstairs and survey the damage. My heart almost stopped in my chest as I surveyed my wrecked house. Two windows were smashed, a chair had been smashed to bits against the wall. Broken plates and nick-knacks littered the floor as far as the eye could see, but what really made my stomach drop was the red spray paint message scrawled across my chimney breast.

You're dead bitch!

I felt sick to my stomach. Not this again! How had they found out where I was so quickly?

I sat in the wreckage for a moment and sobbed until I could sob no more. I thought this was over, I thought I could start afresh somewhere new. How stupid was I? There was no running away was there? Even if I changed my name they'd still find me, somehow.

I got to my feet and wiped away my tears, time to get this mess tidied up. It wasn't the first time I'd been through this and it was starting to look like it wouldn't be the last. The first thing I did was to re-lock the back door. The first crash I'd heard earlier was obviously my back door being kicked in. Although they'd broken the lock in the process, I hadn't remembered to put the slider bolts across when I went to bed, so these were still intact. I slid top and bottom bolts across, feeling a little safer in the process. Next I made my way down the hall to the front door. To my surprise the door was locked and my keys were on the doormat. I picked up the keys and twirled them around my fingers thoughtfully. It seemed the mystery man had locked my front door when he left and posted the keys back through the letter box. It was a strange situation. I stared at the door as I slid the keys into the lock and unlocked it. I pulled my robe around me tightly and peered around the door. I looked up and down the dark and empty street seeing nothing but the dark shapes of vegetation swaying in the breeze. As I was closing the door my eyes fell on the dim shape behind the rhododendron across the street. As I watched, the figure stepped into the light of the gate for a moment locking eyes with me. It was the creep from the coffee shop again. He stared at me for a moment before stepping backwards into the darkness once more leaving me watching shadows dance across my neighbour's lawn. I hurried inside and slammed the door behind me, hands fumbling to turn the key in the lock as fast as I could.

I didn't know what was worse, the predator or the saviour.

There would be no more sleep tonight. I dressed quickly and got to work cleaning up the debris field that used to be my home.

Three hours later and I had the place in some semblance to normality; albeit without as many possessions as I had before, but I had been meaning to go a little more minimalist lately anyway. That would be my excuse should anyone stop by and question my lack of belongings. The graffiti on the wall was not as easy to get rid of. I had scrubbed and scrubbed at it until my hands were sore and I'd barely even faded it. The only solution was to paint over it when I got home from work later, and while I was at the hardware store I would invest in some new locks and a burglar alarm.

Chapter Seven

EXHIBIT G

Oh my love, what a night! I fear for you so much! This is not a safe world that we live in anymore. When you aren't even safe to go to bed without being terrorised something is very wrong. I'll keep watch over you my sweet, I will keep you safe. If I have to give my life to keep you safe, then I will gladly, I know that I will see you on the other side someday, I would wait till the end of the world for you.

The incident with the intruder was so unpleasant and unexpected, I'm just glad that I handled it as well as I did and kept my composure. Things could have so easily got nasty.

Stay safe my sweet…

***

"You look tired." Ruby observed as we made our way out of the office block later that day.

"Yeah, I didn't sleep great that night."

"I'm surprised you can sleep at all with the things that must be on your mind."

"I'll be fine." I replied. "Where do you want to go for lunch?"

"J-J's, they have a special lunch menu on at the minute that's to die for." The words froze on her lips and her cheeks coloured up. I wish she'd stop trying not to say death or die, it's just making things awkward that shouldn't be.

"Sounds good." I said, pretending to not notice her awkwardness. I slid my arm through hers and we meandered through the precinct to the little café that she had suggested.

We managed to get a table quite quickly despite the place being so busy, I think that was probably down to the way the waiter had his hand possessively on her waist when they thought no one was looking.

"Here we are." He said leading us to a table to the side of the aisle.

"Thank you very much." Ruby said, batting her eyes dramatically.

"Oh it's my pleasure, madam."

Jesus I felt like a third wheel.

Once Romeo had gone I felt a little more comfortable and picked up the lunchtime menu to see what I fancied to eat. I was disturbed from my perusing by a familiar voice asking, "Is this seat taken?"

I looked up to see John peering down at us hopefully.

"Course you can!" Ruby exclaimed sliding over. "We don't mind if John sits with us, do we Paula?"

"Erm, no I suppose that's alright."

"It's just that there's no other tables available and by the time I find somewhere else to eat, dinner break will be over." He sat down gratefully.

"You know what?" Ruby suddenly exclaimed, "I've just remembered, I was supposed to pick up my sister's dry-cleaning for her. You know I completely forgot all about it. You don't mind if I just nip off for a bit do you Paula?"

"Not at all." I said through gritted teeth at being so blatantly manipulated into being set up.

She flounced off with a wink and the flip of her hip. I scowled after her briefly wishing for a moment that she would trip over her arse on the way out.

"So…" John began, looking a little flustered. "What's the food like in here?"

"It's fine." I began studying my menu for all it was worth and did my best to ignore him. I heard him clear his throat – trying to get my attention I suppose, but I declined to indulge him. My dinner break was my own and I had no wish to share it with a man I didn't care for and had in no way encouraged.

"Sorry." He whispered.

I looked up despite myself. "Mm?"

"I said I'm sorry."

I wasn't entirely sure how to handle this. "Oh it's okay, I suppose Ruby set you up with this."

"I didn't mean sorry for interrupting your lunch."

"Oh, oh you mean sorry for the other…for googling me you mean?"

He leaned in a little closer to me, almost affectionately before whispering, "No I mean sorry that you're a fucking cold-blooded killer."

My stomach dropped like a stone. "What?"

He moved his face a little closer to mine, I was wedged against the back of the booth so there was no escape. "I know all about you, and I'm here to give you a bit of advice Paula. Run. Leave. I won't warn you again. There's other's looking for you that won't be as kind as me."

I could find no words.

"Last night? That was just a taster, if your bodyguard hadn't shown up, my friend had been told to cut-you-up good. They've been looking for you for a while. Imagine my surprise when I found you here, working in the same office. I really do think it's fate." He grabbed my hand tightly across the table. "David was a good friend of mine. The Judge might've believed your bullshit, but none of us did, and they want blood; they want your blood, and they're going to make you pay."

I snatched my hand away, painfully twisting it in the process. "Leave me alone."

"I am leaving you alone. But the others won't. If you don't run it's not going to be pretty."

I could feel my heart pounding in my eardrums. This fear was like a sickness, I fought to find my voice. "Was that you in my house?"

"No. I just gave them your address. I owe them everything, I owe you jack-shit."

"Please tell them to leave me alone. I didn't do anything. He was going to kill me. I loved him so much, I…." I felt me voice break as the tears started to flow.

"Bullshit. Crocodile tears won't work with me." He stared at me with amusement. "Are you done? You think you've got something to cry about now? Just wait, just you fucking wait."

My breath caught in my throat as an awful thought occurred to me. "Does Ruby know about this?"

He shook his head smiling. "No, she thinks I fancy you. Ha!"

"Are you ready to order?" The waiter interrupted loudly dropping a basket of bread in front of us. I quickly wiped my eyes and tried to hide behind my menu.

"Why yes, I think we are," John beamed, handing his menu to the waiter. "I think we'll both have the steak, rare."

Chapter Eight

I took the afternoon off claiming that I had a migraine. It wasn't a complete lie, after all my head was spinning. One thing was for certain, I couldn't stay here, I'd have to move again and this time change my name, maybe even my appearance. I'd been a fool thinking I could just move on with my life, that my past wouldn't chase me down like a dog.

I let myself into my house for what was probably the last time. The message from my intruder screamed out at me from the chimney breast – bleeding its way down the wall and into my brain. I turned back to the front door and locked it quickly, taking a moment to get my breath back and gather my composure, heart attacks were prolific in my family and the way my own was dancing double-quick I surely would be next in line to follow the trend.

I caught sight of my answer machine flashing from its place on the sideboard. With a decisive stride I pulled the plug from the wall. Every day I unplugged the blasted thing yet time after time I found it plugged back in, smugly blinking at me from the dark. I had been starting to think my house was haunted, now though I knew better. Frankly a ghost is the more pleasant of the two explanations.

The first thing I did was to check that every door and window was still closed tightly, feeling my stomach do a little dip as I realised that my kitchen window was in the closed position but not actually locked. I banged the handle down quickly whilst looking around me for any sign of an intruder. After a careful examination of the house I concluded that I was alone and with every door and window firmly bolted I was reasonably safe…for now.

I made myself a cup of tea and took it upstairs to my bedroom - the only place I felt safe. I closed the door and slid a chair under the handle for good measure. After placing my cup down on my dressing table I found myself seated on the stool in front of it -staring at my own haunted eyes across the glass. I took a moment to really look at myself, to see myself as I am, not as I imagine I am. "You're a fool, that's what you are," my reflection told me with a shake of her head.

"I know," I replied.

I turned away from her accusing stare and tried to gather my thoughts. Where could I go where they wouldn't find me? For Christs-sake I didn't even know who 'they' were. And how would I fund my escape? I had barely a penny saved.

I sank down onto my bed and pulled out my book from under my pillow. Ruby had touched on something the previous evening when she had suggested I should sell my story. As I told her, I would never trust the tabloids again, but that didn't mean that I hadn't been writing my own side of the story. Even if I never dare send it to a publisher, at least my thoughts on the matter would be recorded in print by my own hand. I picked up the black ball-point pen from my bedside table and began to record the latest events. Even as I began to write I knew I was just stalling. I should be packing; I should be running.

***

I must've nodded off over my book as it was dark when I came to my senses and realised my mobile phone was ringing. Through foggy eyes I grasped it from the nightstand and croaked "Hello?"

"Hey, it's me," Ruby said.

I sat up a bit and flicked my lamp on whilst trying to organise my sleepy brain.

"Hi." I replied.

"Are you coming out tonight?"

"No, I don't really feel like it tonight. Thanks though."

"I won't take no for an answer."

I grated my teeth at the unwelcome intrusion. "I can't tonight Ruby, I'm not even home."

"Well you better be in because I'm standing outside your house and I just saw a light go on in your bedroom. If that isn't you then you have a problem."

Damn-it! "Okay, yes it's me, I am in, I just don't feel good."

"All the better to let Aunty Ruby in then."

I huffed and glared at the ceiling. "Fine. Hang on a sec." I cancelled the call and padded downstairs to let her in. Just what I needed!

"Look at the state of you!" She tutted as she pushed past me into the hallway.

"Come in." I offered her departing shadow.

"I'm in need of alcohol and company." She admitted, biting her bottom lip.

My nerves were in overdrive as I stood looking at her, backlit by the hate message on my chimney breast through the open doorway, she -oblivious to her halo of red paint and hate. "Why, what's wrong?" I asked, anxiously looking from her to the message, hoping that she wouldn't turn and see it.

"Because I just made a complete fool of myself and you're probably going to hate me for it too, but I don't really have that many friends these days so here I am…to confess."

I felt my blood run a little cold.

"I made a pass at Mr Dreamboat earlier after I left you at lunch." She stared at me trying to gauge my reaction.

I'm well-rehearsed at masking my emotions, so I hid my fury and desire to punch her face in. I said nothing and let her prattle on.

"He knocked me back, by the way, just so you know. I found out his name though, he's called Karl, with a K." She smiled nervously down at her feet. "To be honest I think he's a bit soft in the head, he was coming out with all sorts of rubbish before he scarpered. He wasn't at all what I expected him to be, got a proper bee in his bonnet. And I'm sorry I threw you at John earlier. It was my stupid attempt to try and distract you from Karl. How did that go by the way?" She looked up hopefully.

"It didn't go well, put it that way."

"Oh…Well I *am* sorry; I don't know what I was thinking."

I knew what I was thinking, I could throttle her for the trouble she'd caused me, setting me up with that psycho.

"Do you want to come out for a drink? Commiserate about what bastards men are?"

"No."

"Aw come on, let me make it up to you. I know the bouncer at that swanky new club that just opened. You know, the one opposite our office block? Come on, I know you've been dying to go for ages."

She was right, I had been dying to go for ages, but that was the last thing on my mind. Now all that mattered was staying safe. I looked at her pouting lips and wondered for the umpteenth time how I could've befriended her, she was not my sort of person at all really. I could never confide in her about what was happening to me, she either wouldn't understand, or even worse, she'd tip the press off about me. She started to turn around sighing as she did so – which made me panic as I did not want her to see what was written across my wall. I thought fast on my feet and reached out and grabbed her in a hug and said quickly – "Course I forgive you and yes, I will come out tonight. Now come upstairs and help me decide what to wear."

She hugged me back and giggled excitedly, not realising I was reaching behind her and pulling the living room door shut. I could've wrung her neck but needs-must. Plus, from a safety point of view – at least I was going to a busy crowded place. Perhaps that was better than sitting alone waiting for the inevitable to happen while I desperately tried to think of somewhere to runaway to. I'd have to keep my wits about me though, no drinking, at all.

***

EXHIBIT H

You know, sometimes I hate you. I hate you that you've turned my world upside down like this. I can't think of anything but you, let alone function properly anymore. I shall spend tonight watching you again, keeping vigil over you, keeping you safe from intruders - and I am well aware that they are at the gate!

Oh if we had never met! My life might still be my own. It is a physical thing this pain, this longing, this...ache. I try to see you all the time, but life seems to present hurdles between us, as if it means to hold us apart. But that's not how it's going to be...you are my destiny, as I am yours, and I will move heaven and earth my love, ours is no idle and trite soppy love story, we are...we are...we ARE!

Chapter Nine

I didn't care for the way that Ruby was behaving tonight. Something was really...*off* with her. She flirted non-stop with anything in trousers yet kept one eye on me constantly as if to gauge my reaction. She could do whatever she wanted as far as I was concerned, I'm not her mother or her keeper. I was a little relieved when she left me for the dancefloor for a while, it meant I could slink into a dark corner, unobserved and discreet to watch the room around me without having to make small talk and pretend to be enjoying myself.

I wasn't. This was simply a necessary exercise in safety.

From my place in the corner I spotted Karl - Mr Dreamboat approaching the bar just ahead of me and felt my heart skip a little beat as I saw him emerging through the parting crowd. He seemed to feel my stare and turned to look at me. For a brief moment our gaze locked and I saw a strange look in his eyes as they flashed from my eyes to my lips. What was that look? Need, want, hunger? He turned away quickly leaving me feeling as though a door had just slammed shut, leaving me out in the cold. It was very dark in here, had I mistaken that look?

Before I could stop myself I found my feet being pulled towards him. Stealing my way across the crowded bar I wove in and out of people before finding myself to within grasping distance of him. I stared at the curve of his back as I stood behind him, revelling in the scent that came off his body, marvelling in how close I was to laying my hands on him. I was just reaching out a hand to gently tap him on the shoulder when a hand grabbed my arm roughly.

"Hey!" I yelled, as I turned to try and free myself from the iron-like grasp. I found myself face-to face with the creep from the coffee shop. "Let go!" I wrestled my arm free as he stood there glaring at me. He looked so out of place and uncomfortable standing there in the middle of the crowded bar full of bright-young-things clad in sequins and silk, he dressed in polyester and Brylcreem. He continued to glare at me even as people continued to barge into him in an effort to get to the bar.

"What's your problem?" I yelled, trying to make myself heard over the loud music.

He pointed at me, finger and thumb in pistol fashion. "You know!"

"Leave me alone."

"Leave him alone!" He countered. "You know better!"

I backed away from him, accidently bumping into a girl causing her to spill her drink.

"Look where you're going!" She yelled, looking down to make sure none landed on her dress.

"I'm so sorry," I gushed. "Please, let me buy you another."

I turned to look back at my stalker to find that he'd vanished into the crowd.

"Creep." I whispered to myself.

"Him again!" Ruby bellowed in my ear as she flung her arms around me as she twirled her way off the dancefloor. "He has serious issues that one. You mark my words. I'd keep right away from him," she finished with a stern frown and a wave of her finger.

***

Ruby and I shared a taxi home once she was finally persuaded to leave. Unfortunately her home was closer to the club than mine so it meant that once she was dropped off - I was left alone in the taxi with my thoughts and fears. I'd tried a little small talk with the taxi driver to ease my nerves but he only answered my awkward questions with a grunt, so I gave up and fell back into awkward silence.

The dark world seemed to fly by my window in a wave of ominous black, peppered with a flicker of electric light that did little to ease my worried mind. Through the daylight hours I could brazen out my fears but at night they came knocking at my windowpane.

As the taxi started to pull towards the road that would bring me to my home my nerves got the better off me.

"Could you stop here please?" I asked, undoing my belt and pulling my purse from out of my pocket. "Here will do." I ordered.

The taxi driver flashed his eyes to mine in the rear-view mirror and indicated to pull in without saying a word.

"How much?"

He tapped to the digital screen on his dashboard without a word and held out his hand.

"Keep the change." I bundled the money into his hand and quickly got out. I'd barely closed the door when he sped off into the night leaving me shrouded in the red of his tail-lights.

I was suddenly very alone. Alone, but relieved. The thought of going back into that house in the dark, alone, not knowing who was in there or what they'd do to me, was just too much. I may be out in the dark late at night, but at least I had a fighting chance. I decided to go for a discrete late-night walk, once the daylight broke in a few hours, then I'd go home.

***

EXHIBIT I

I waited outside your house for hours. Where were you? Oh how I worry for you my darling. I'm simply going to have to speed things up, I can't go on like this, you break my heart so. I don't have the luxury of time anymore, I can't wait for you to notice me, I'll have to MAKE YOU NOTICE ME!

Seeing you in that seedy club earlier was just too much. I could see the way you were being leered at - even if you pretended not to notice. What were you doing in a place like that? It doesn't become you!

Forgive me my darling, you just make me so angry sometimes. You mess with my head as well as my heart. I simply can't go on like this. I have decided, tonight is the night. Tonight is the night that we are going to unite. This is it. I can barely breath as the flood of love for you pulsing through my veins is so...intense. Look at what you do to me - without even trying. You intoxicate me.

Until tonight....xxx

***

As dawn broke I slid the key into my front door and took a deep breath as I slowly pushed the door open. I was prepared for anything this time. I was cold, tired, dirty and found myself too exhausted to be frightened. I was ready to face anything and anybody in order to get this ordeal over and done with so that I could go to bed and sleep for a decade or two.

Nothing was too obvious from the hallway; I could see no sign of forced entry. Mm. I stared at the living room door for a moment before quickly turning the handle and throwing the door open. I stepped into the room in disbelief as I took in the neat and tidy room looking exactly as I had left it. What was going on?

After exploring the house top to bottom I had to conclude that I'd had a brief reprieve and to be perfectly honest, I wasn't sure if I was happy about it. The endless waiting for something to happen was worse than any fate that had been planned for me.

My imagination was a dark place.

After checking that every door and window was locked once again – I clambered up the stairs to my bedroom. I shook my shoes off, slid my bag off my shoulder and took out my notebook from the side pouch before clambering -fully dressed – into bed. I would sleep while I could and preserve what was left of my strength for later. I had to depart soon.

Chapter Ten

EXHIBIT J

Now is the time my darling. I can wait no more. I spent the daylight hours sleeping and dreaming of you and now I've come to take my prize....

I know you're home, I saw the light on in your bathroom. I shan't bother knocking, knocking is for strangers, I'm not a stranger, I'm your lover, I'm coming home, I'm always welcome...

***

I lingered for a while, hidden in the shrubbery across the road from your house. I was a little unsure of how I would explain and declare myself to you, I wanted to get it just right...it was important.

I warmed my hands for a moment against the glass of the lantern seated upon your neighbour's gate thinking to myself that this was the last time I would be skulking around in the shrubbery watching from the fringes of your life. From now on I would BE your life.

No more time for delays, it was time. But perhaps I would knock first after all...

***

The knocking on the door took my breath away. Such things shouldn't be so scary, this was ridiculous. I peered through the glass pane of the back door, seeing no-one except my own reflection. With a sigh I pulled out the key from my back pocket and slid it into the lock, reached out and unlocked the back door with shaking hands. I opened it slowly, looking around as I did so. I seemed to be alone, but I knew that couldn't be the case.

"Hello?" I called.

"What the hell?" A voice bellowed from behind me. "I told you, you can't be here!"

I turned to see Karl standing in the doorway glaring at me. Before I could speak he pulled a small device from his pocket and pressed a button.

"What was that?" I stammered in panic.

"It's my panic button, my security guard will be here any minute so don't go trying anything, just turn around and leave. NOW!"

"But I love you David."

"We've been through this; my name isn't David it's Karl. I don't know how the hell you got in here but you can just turn around right now."

"I've got a key."

"How the hell did you get a key Paula?"

"When you left your kitchen window open for me I came in and took the spare key you'd left out for me."

"I knew you'd be in the house again! You took my photos, my jewellery, didn't you?"

"But they're not just yours, they belong to both of us, what's mine is yours and what's yours is mine. You know that." I started walking softly towards him, I just wanted to hold him. For him to wrap his arms around me and tell me that everything would be alright. I've waited so long...

"Get back, you're crazy, you know that?" He started backing away from me looking for something to grab I think. What was wrong with him? He grabbed a sweeping brush and held it out in front of him like a weapon.

"Stop being so silly," I chided. "Is this some type of game? Are you into role-play or something? You've never mentioned it before."

I turned, startled by the sound of the backdoor flying open.

"Stop right there!" It was my creepy stalker.

"God, leave me alone will you. Why do you keep following me everywhere I go? What the hell are you doing here?"

He started approaching me slowly causing me to back up a little. I didn't trust him.

"I have been retained by Karl to keep an eye on you, make sure you weren't violating your restraining order."

I sneered; he was so stupid. "Oh please, those things aren't worth the paper they're written on."

"I know," the creep said, "that's why I'm here. Now I did you a favour the other night and got rid of that yobbo that was gonna hurt you, how about you do me a favour now and go home and leave Karl in peace?"

"Don't be stupid. I am home, I live here now. Today's the day I move in." I pulled out my notebook from my bag and turned to the last page. I folded it over and held it up for the creep to see.

... I know you're home, I saw the light on in your bathroom. I shan't bother knocking, knocking is for strangers, I'm not a stranger, I'm your lover, I'm coming home, I'm always welcome...

"See, it say's I'm coming home and I'm always welcome." I slammed the book shut with a satisfied smirk. I'm no fool, I know I have my facts right - I have *evidence*.

"But *you* wrote that." The creep said.

"No I didn't." I countered.

"You did!"

"I didn't, *fate* wrote it. Our destiny was written in the starts and in the hearts and minds of David and I."

"Karl! My name is Karl you stupid bitch!"

Ouch, that hurt and made me wince. "You shouldn't talk to me like that. It's not nice."

I could see them both trying to gesture to each other while they thought I wasn't looking, I didn't like that, it felt like they were plotting against me. I'd waited too long for this moment and I wasn't going to let them spoil it. I put the notebook back in my bag and pulled out the small revolver I'd managed to buy from a 'friend of a friend'. They looked quite startled I thought as I cocked the pistol and pointed it at them. I was still a little wounded from the harsh tone that David had used on me. I'd have to get him trained in better manners now that we're living together. "Now go sit down quietly in there." I gestured with the gun in the direction of the living room.

"Look, let's just talk about this for a minute…" The creep started.

"I'm done talking, now get in there and sit quietly before I shoot you in the kneecaps."

He clamped up pretty quick then and gestured for David to follow him through to the living room. They both sat down on the couch staring at me fearfully.

"Now just stay quiet for a few minutes while I update my notebook."

***

...Oh my love, our happy ever after is here! I knew you'd love me if you just let me in. I see how much you adore me by the look of love in your eyes. You feel what I feel, don't you David? Other's may conspire to separate us...but that can't happen again, not now, we've gone too far. Till death us do part...

Chapter Eleven

The creep was going to have to go, this would not do at all. How could David and I have any quality time with *that creep* sitting on our sofa watching our every move? To be honest he looked like he was making David very uncomfortable. As I watched my love, I could see the tension in his shoulders and in his hands - fidgeting away there against the restraints I had lovingly placed there.

I couldn't have my love made to feel threatened like this.

"You," I addressed the creep, "you can't stay here. You've outstayed your welcome and it's time for you to go."

He looked like he would've replied if he hadn't had his mouth taped shut. I could see in his body language what he would say to me, if he could, and that was a lot of lies and profanity I had no desire to hear. I positioned my revolver to his head to have a better chance of getting him to behave. "Stand up," I ordered.

He reluctantly obliged, glaring at me as he did so.

I waved my gun towards the staircase meaningfully. He looked from me to the staircase and back to the barrel of my gun again before slowly edging his way to the staircase.

"Now climb!"

I had to stick the gun into his back a few times to get him to climb the stairs without dragging his heels so grudgingly. "Now in there." I pointed to the airing cupboard just in front of him. It looked as though there used to be an old immersion hot-water tank in there at some point in the house's history but that had long since gone, leaving a tall, empty, narrow cupboard just large enough for the creep to stand up in.

He started mumbling through the tape over his mouth again, no doubt some load of rubbish that wouldn't interest me very much. I slid my revolver down and rested it against his crotch and whispered, "Now pretty please, get in the cupboard."

With no more protests he backed into the tight space, staring at me as I swung the door shut and slid the bolt across, leaving him in the darkness to think about the consequences of his actions. For good measure, I then nailed the door shut.

Good. Out of sight, out of mind. As far as I care now, the creep has moved on to pastures new leaving me and my David in blessed peace at last.

I made my way back into the living room with a new spring in my step. Gosh, I was just so happy! I sat down on David's knee and wrapped my arms about him, resting my head against his chest and breathing him in. "I love you so much my sweetheart." I whispered in his ear as I stroked his hair.

His muffled reply sounded as if he said, "Don't let me go."

"I won't my darling, not ever."

***

It was such a tear to leave him and go to work, but needs must. While David was relaxing at home I would be the bread winner, bringing home the crust for the man I love. I positively skipped to work; I was so happy!

"What are you grinning at?" Ruby demanded as I sat down at my desk.

"Nothing," I shrugged nonchalantly, "just having a good day, that's all."

"Mm."

***

"So do you want to come out tonight?" Ruby asked as she hurried over to me as I was leaving work.

"Nope, I'm looking forward to a night in." I carried on walking; I had no wish to get caught up in any of Ruby's nonsense today.

"You're up to something." She observed, chasing after me a little to keep up. "Wait a minute, you've got a fella."

I stopped and turned to her. "Maybe." I couldn't help the grin that spread across my face.

"Who is it? Do I know him?"

"You could say that."

"John? I thought you didn't like him."

"No not John."

"So who else could it…oh, you don't mean…not Karl? Not Mr Dreamboat himself?"

I just grinned at her. She'd used his old name but I'd forgive her on this occasion.

"How the hell did that come about? Because I tell you, that day I made a play for him he came out with a right load of rubbish, told me to tell *you* to stop hounding him. I told him he was a nut-job if he thought you having a tiny little crush on him counted as stalking him. He sounded like a complete lunatic to me."

I shook my head. "We've been seeing each other for a while now, in secret. He was just trying to throw you off the scent, we weren't ready to go public yet and he panicked."

She didn't look convinced, but she was just jealous. She wanted what I had, and she could get lost, he was mine!

"So you see, I really can't come out with you tonight. I'm heading out to *Ann Summers* first to get something to spice things up, and then it's an early night for me." I gave what I hoped was a cheeky wink.

She was still staring at me,

"What?"

She shook her head and exhaled slowly. "Nothing I suppose." She pulled her handbag up over her shoulder and started to fidget. "Well I guess I'll see you Monday then."

"Yep, see you Monday."

I stood and stared after her for a moment as she ran to catch a bus. I smiled. "Why would he want *you* when he has *me?*" I stood for a few more moments before turning and heading for *Ann Summers*.

***

I'd never been in a shop like this before and felt quite nervous as I made my way inside. I could feel my cheeks burning already and I hadn't even viewed anything yet. I had a brief look at the website the previous day and so I knew that they had the items I needed in stock.

Looking up at the signs above the aisles I eventually spotted the bondage section. Good.

My goodness, there were things in there that made me cross my legs with fear. There must be some strange people that enjoy attaching clamps to themselves.

After wandering a little further I found the restraints that I was looking for. I looked about me to make sure no-one was watching as I pulled them off the hanger and took a closer look. They looked like nylon trusses from what I could see on the packaging – which should be just the job. I slid the packet down into my basket and put my handbag in there on top of it so that no-one could peek at what I was buying. Next on my list was the ball-gag which I found quite easily. I finished off by adding a black hood to my basket, then after a little debate – a whip.

David and I would be having a very busy weekend.

***

EXHIBIT L

…The sweetest feeling in the world is to love and be loved. Oh how I adore you! I wake for you, live for you, bleed for you. How could we ever survive without each other now? I couldn't and I won't…

Chapter Twelve

I had to stop by my old house on my way home to collect more of my things. I didn't like returning to the place where I felt so unsafe, so persecuted. I felt the hair on the back of my neck rise a little as I slid my key into the front door and felt the key click around uselessly. The lock was broken. Someone had forced the lock and broken it. My god, someone had been inside again. Oh my, what if they were still there?

I backed away from the front door a little, looking up at the house. I could see nothing through any of the windows, no shadows or shapes that shouldn't be there. I was just trying to decide whether to dare go inside or not when my next-door neighbour came out to call in his cat.

"Eccles!" He bellowed, "Eccles! Come on you little sod!" He turned to me suddenly noticing my presence. "Hiya love, are you alright? You look a bit peaky."

I pointed to my front door. "Someone's broken in. I don't know if they're still in there or not. I daren't go in."

He pulled his own front door shut behind him and hopped over the low wall into my garden. He shook his head as he looked at my lock. "This used to be a nice neighbourhood this you know. This never would've happened at one time. We used to have neighbourhood watch! Do you want me to go in? Make sure there's no-one inside?"

I was so relieved. "Would you?"

"Of course!" He puffed out his chest, wiped his hands together with a slight bravado, I thought, and then pushed open the door.

I hopped from one foot to the other while I waited for him to return. What if there was someone in there? What if he got hurt? It would be all my fault.

I was extremely relieved when he returned a few minutes later. "All clear." He held the door a little wider so I could follow him in. "It's a mess though," he warned, shaking his head. "I don't think there's anything missing as far as I can see, but they've sure made a mess."

My heart sank as I took in the graffiti that now covered most of the walls of my home.

Murdering Bitch, Gonna fucking slit your throat

Everywhere I turned there were more sick threats screaming out at me from the walls. I sank to the floor as my knees gave way. I could feel my eyes filling up with tears and my throat was getting tight from the sob that was trying to escape.

"Now, now," my neighbour said gently. "Come on, there's no need for tears, you can't let horrible bastards like this get to you. If you do that then you've won. Come on, come next door with me and have a cup of tea, steady your nerves a bit and then I'll see to fixing that front door for you."

I couldn't speak for the lump that had formed in my throat, so I nodded and allowed him to escort me back out of the house and into his cosy kitchen next-door.

I couldn't help but notice my answer machine plugged back in and blinking away as I left.

***

"Here you go, get that down you." My neighbour placed a hot cup of tea in front of me.

"Thank you…I'm sorry I don't even know your name."

"Barry," he held his hand out to shake mine with a smile, "pleased to meet ya."

"I'm Paula." I stared down into my tea before taking a grateful sip, gasping a little as it was very hot.

"Yeah, it's alright love I knew your name already. Don't take this the wrong way, but…I… erm…remember seeing you on the news and stuff." He looked bashfully at me.

"Oh." I felt my cheeks colouring again. Whenever I thought I'd left my past behind me it came hurtling out at unexpected times. "What they were saying about me, it wasn't true, none of it. The jury knew straight away that I was innocent." I stared down into my tea quickly. I felt cornered again.

"It was a nasty business that." He shook his head sagely. "Poor little thing like you getting dragged through the gutter-press like that before anyone knew the facts. By, you went through it didn't 'ya lass. And to think people wonder why women such as yourself are too scared to ask for help when they're getting hell at home from their fellas." He shook his head again. "You deserve a bloody medal for what you went through with that bastard. I remember the details that came out after the trial, he'd kept you as a prisoner for months, hadn't he?"

I nodded.

"It happened to my old mum you know. She put up with my dad beating her for nigh on thirty-five years before she snapped and fought back. Wacked him over the head with a frying pan she did, damn nearly killed him. But things were kept behind closed doors in them days. Even when the police got wind of it, they never prosecuted her, just told him to mend his ways or they'd let her finish him off."

I smiled a little. It was nice to have some sympathy for a change. People never knew just how I'd suffered.

He continued, "Is that what all *that's* about next-door then? People sticking their noses in where it doesn't belong, stirring up trouble?"

I nodded. "Something like that."

"Well don't you worry love, me and the wife, we'll look after you. You've only to bang on the wall and I'll be straight round with my baseball bat."

I smiled a real smile. "I'll remember that."

***

Once I finished my tea I went back into my house to gather together the things that I would need to help my relationship with David. As I gathered up my books and a few clothes I could hear Barry whistling to himself downstairs while he was fixing the lock on my front door. I hadn't had the heart to tell him that I wouldn't be spending much time here anymore, not now David and I had decided to start living together. However, the rent was paid up for the next three months so I might as well keep the place on - to store my furniture if nothing else. Eventually David and I would decide on which furniture to keep, after all, we had two houses full of furniture between us. It would take some sorting out and some compromises from us both, but I don't mind compromising, as long as David's happy, I'm happy.

"I'm all finished love!" Barry called up the stairs.

"Brilliant, thanks Barry." I took one last look through the books I had piled up to put in my little suitcase and smiled. Yes, you could keep your self-help books and your relationship books. I had better books than that, I had practical books with practical solutions. I picked up the first book – *'Reincarnation – lost past lives,'* followed by - *'Animal behaviour – Training guide.'* Next on the pile was – *'Animal training 101.'* Followed by *'Perfect response training.'* The last book on my pile was a guide for training Falcons - through diet, weight control and a process called 'manning' which I believed meant spending a lot of time with your animal to get them accustomed to – and used to your presence. I had happened upon the latter book quite by accident, although after reading it through, it made quite a lot of sense and so I had decided to implement quite a lot of the teachings that it suggested.

I slid the books into my case, pulled out the clothes I would need for the week ahead, and after a cursory look around my graffiti-covered room, I departed.

Onwards and upwards!

Chapter Thirteen

As I wheeled my little suitcase towards my new home I noticed to my horror someone banging on my new front door. I felt my stomach do a little somersault. It was probably something perfectly innocent, I told myself. But I was very wary as I made my way up the path towards the stranger.

"Sorry. Do you live here?" He asked, turning to me.

He looked fairly unthreatening, so I came a little closer. "Yes, I just moved in with my boyfriend. Why, can I help you with something?"

"Well I'm sorry to intrude Miss, it's just that I live next-door and there's been an awful banging coming from your house all day, it's been driving me round the twist. Got the builders in have you? Anyway, I just wondered what all the noise was about."

"Oh, I'm ever so sorry, I can't think what that could be." I bit my bottom lip thoughtfully. I'll just pop inside and see what's going on." I slid past him apologetically and let myself in, closing the door behind me. As soon as I entered I knew what the neighbour meant. I could hear a strange banging myself.

I decided to investigate.

The noise seemed to be coming from upstairs, so I put my suitcase down and made my way up there first. I opened my bedroom door first and saw that David was still tied to the bed where I'd left him, bless him, he looked so sweet laid there. His eyes were smiling at me even though his lips were hidden from view by the tape, I blew him a little kiss as I closed the door. I stood listening for a moment on the landing. The noise seemed to be coming from the airing cupboard across from my bedroom. I took a closer look at the door, running my fingers over the little slider bolt. I wrestled with the stiff bolt and tried to open the door, but it was stuck fast. After a moment I spotted a few shiny nail heads dotted about sporadically – as though the door was nailed shut. Strange. Never mind, I laughed and shook my head as it dawned on me what the noise behind the door must be. I almost skipped down the stairs with relief to go inform my neighbour what the noise was.

I flung the door open startling him in the process. "It's coming from the airing cupboard, it must be the immersion heater making all that racket, there must be something wrong with the hot water."

"Oh, yep, that'd do it." He replied. "I got rid of mine years ago because the damned thing was so noisy. Take my advice love, get a combi-boiler."

"I will do, thanks." I paused. "I'm really sorry for the noise, I promise I'll put a stop to it as soon as possible."

"Appreciated that is love. To be honest, I'm not going to be here for the next fortnight, I'm jetting off to Benidorm in the morning. Can't bloody wait, I can tell you. So don't go worrying about me. I just wondered if you were having building work done that's all. I once had a bad experience with a neighbour that spent two years having building work done. Drove me round the twist! Made me a bit paranoid about noisy neighbours." He gave a little laugh to play down his warning, but I got his warning loud and clear – make noise and I'll give you trouble.

I didn't want trouble. I wanted a quiet life. "Benidorm eh? That sounds lovely."

"Aye, I can't wait for it that's for sure." He started to turn away, "Well, best go start packing eh?"

"Have a lovely time!" I called after the departing figure. I closed the door with a bump and locked it. Gosh what a day for neighbours! I took a moment to collect my thoughts. Cocking my head to one side I could still hear the banging going on upstairs, though maybe not quite as loud as before. I'd give it a few days, see if the problem fixed itself before I started the rigmarole of trying to get a plumber. God only knew how much it would cost to get a new boiler fitted. At least the nosey neighbour was going away for a few weeks, so there was only me to get irritated by the noise, and to be honest – it didn't really bother me. As long as it didn't bother my David, then everything was tickety-boo.

I picked up my heavy case and carried it upstairs to my new bedroom. I could see David gazing adoringly at me as I entered the room. See, he does love me, he's just a little bit confused at the moment, but that's understandable; it's not his fault that he doesn't remember his previous life with me…but he will. His soul remembers me even if his memory is a little hazy.

I opened the large wardrobe across from the bed and took an assessing look at the mass of clothes before me. This was no good, he'd certainly have to have a clear out so that I could fit my clothes in there. I shoved the clothes to one side leaving me a gap of about a foot to hang up my own clothes. It wasn't much, but at least I could hang up the essentials for now. I heaved the pile of books out of the case and set to filling up the wardrobe.

Once I was satisfied that everything was put away neatly, I pulled out of the bottom of the case the carrier bag containing the restraints. I took the bag and emptied the contents onto the bed before sitting down next to David. I pulled my legs up under me and rested my back against the headboard. I liked that our shoulders were touching. I think that David must've got a little static shock off me - as he jumped when our shoulders connected.

He looked very interested in the items that I was examining, his eyes looked quite excited when he saw the ball-gag. I wonder if my David had a kinky side that I didn't know about? Well, they say you never really know anyone until you've lived with them, don't they?

I held it up in front of him. "This will be kinder to your mouth than the tape. I don't want the tape I used on you to chafe your skin. This will keep your skin perfect." I pulled my revolver out from my handbag as a precaution. "Now, I'm going to remove the tape and fit this ball-gag on you instead. Now do us both a favour, and stay quiet. It won't do either of us any good to go attracting attention. We just want a quiet life now, don't we?" I waved the gun lovingly at him.

He nodded his head, completely understanding where I'm coming from.

With my free hand I carefully peeled the heavy-duty tape from his mouth, cringing as it must've been stinging him. "I'm so sorry about that my love."

He took a big gasp of air as the tape finally came off. "Why are you doing this to me? Please, you have to let me go…"

"Shhh." I silenced him with a wave of my gun. "No talking now, that's for later."

I'd never fitted a ball-gag before so it took a bit of figuring out knowing which straps to tighten. Eventually I figured it out. Although I think David must have a darker side in the bedroom, when I tried to fit the ball-gag the first time he tried to bite me. Now I'm not one for biting in the bedroom, that's not really my thing. But we all make sacrifices for the people we love, don't we? So, I compromised and bit him quite hard on the shoulder. He really must be into that sort of thing because he gasped with pleasure.

I became aware of a loud knocking sound again coming from the landing.

If this went on much longer I'd have to get a new boiler.

***

EXHIBIT M

…It's so nice to be close to you like this again. I've missed you so much while we were apart. I just knew you'd come back to me. A love like ours could never die.

I see a little confusion in your eyes at times, I suppose it must be strange for you my love, you remember me, yet you don't remember me, I think you just need time…

Chapter Fourteen

Once I knew that David was safely tethered-up in a kinder way I decided that I should make him something nice to eat. To be honest I'd forgotten all about food until my stomach started growling, reminding me that neither David or I had eaten today. After a careful inspection of my new kitchen I decided to make David's favourite – chicken curry. I hummed to myself as I set about making it. It was so nice to be cooking again for my man.

Once I was satisfied that the curry could be left to simmer, I got myself comfortable in the living room with my books. I intended to absorb everything that I could from these books over the weekend. I planned to start with the reincarnation book – as I believed this would give me the best foundation to start from – followed by the behavioural training books. I was a little unclear about how reincarnation works and was hoping that this book might clarify things a little. Previously to my experience with David, I believed that people who died passed their souls on to the next generation via a new vessel such as a new-born baby. I never knew that one could pass on their soul to someone who was already well established in this world such as David's new body was. Then again, they say God works in mysterious ways. God, Allah, Buddha, or whoever it may be. I knew David was back as soon as I saw Karl's vessel. I just knew it; I could see David's soul shining out from him. I knew he'd come back, somehow. The problem -so I read- is that people don't generally remember their past lives, which is a major obstacle for me, because

I'm determined to bring David's memory back, BY ANY MEANS NECCESARY.

After quickly flicking through the reincarnation book without finding any satisfactory answers I found myself with the Falcon training manual. Now this one made interesting reading. The other animal behaviour books were all about basic training. This book wasn't just about basic training, it also discussed – in depth – *taming*. Now *that* was more like it!

The first step in training the falcon was a process called 'manning' which entailed getting the bird accustomed to your presence. Apparently in the old days, falconers would sit in a darkened room by candle-light to try and settle the bird as much as possible. Once the bird got comfortable it would show its contentment by going to sleep, 'rousing' (shaking it's feathers out) or by sitting on one leg. I could certainly sit in the darkened bedroom with David as much as he needed if it would help him feel more relaxed. I turned back to the book. The next stage in training was getting the bird to eat whilst sitting on your fist, a process that could take many days determined by the individual bird's stubbornness. The process of training a bird wasn't to starve the bird into submission, the bird could eat as much as it wanted, it just had to eat with the falconer. And so, the battle of wills would commence.

I thought about the curry I had simmering away in the kitchen. This would be an ideal time to start his training process, he was already hungry, he must be. He hadn't eaten for two days. I'd have to put my new knowledge into practice. Let David know he can eat whatever he wants - just as long as he does something for me first.

***

"Now what is your name?"

"Karl," he croaked through cracked lips. "Please…"

"No." I held the spoon of curry away from his lips. "Try again, what's your name?"

"Karl."

"DAVID!" I yelled and threw the spoon down into the dish. "No dinner till you start getting the questions right. WHAT IS YOUR NAME?"

Silence.

He stared at me with his mouth clamped firmly shut.

If he wanted a battle of wills he could have one. "You'll get nothing to eat if you don't cooperate."

He stared at me unblinking. After a moment, he croaked out. "Water."

I picked up a glass of water off the tray that I'd brought up and held it up in front of him. "And who wants the drink of water?"

He looked pained for a moment.

"WHO wants the drink of water, tell me?"

"…David."

I was delighted. Progress, at last! "See, was that really so hard?" I held the glass to his lips while he drank and I stroked his hair sweetly.

"Now," I began as I took the water away. "Would you like some food?"

He nodded.

"And what is your name?"

"David."

"Excellent."

***

I was pleased with David's progress, to be honest I was surprised that it was so easy. I had expected more of a battle of wills, but perhaps that's because he knows deep down who he really is anyway. I wondered if he was relieved in a way?

I left the bedroom with the tray balanced in on one arm while I closed the door behind me. I stopped suddenly as I heard that pesky boiler starting to bang again. Not quite as loud as before but still very annoying. Well it was a new house, I supposed, all houses seem to have strange noises at first to you get used to the funny little creaks and bumps.

After a mentally draining day I finally settled down to my own dinner – which was now cold, but never mind. Nothing could shake my happiness.

Chapter Fifteen

One thing that hadn't really occurred to me, David would need bathroom breaks. I didn't realise my oversight until the next morning when I woke up next to him feeling damp and sticky. "What the hell?" I asked, flinging the covers back in confusion.

David was looking pale and stressed so I think he must've been embarrassed.

"Oh my. This won't do, this won't do at all." I looked about me in a panic. What should I do? I couldn't very well remake the bedding with David still tied to the bed, could I? If I untied him would he stay?

Course he would. I pulled my gun out from the bedside table.

"Now I'm going to untie you and let you use the toilet and take a bath. Once I'm satisfied that you're clean, I'm going to stand guard while *you* change the sheets. I don't want any trouble David, do you understand?"

After a moment he nodded. I noticed a little tear roll down his left cheek, poor David, I'd be mortified too if I'd just wet the bed.

"Now I mean it, no funny business. We've come too far now to go and spoil it by doing something silly." I held the gun in my right hand whilst I undid the ball-gag with my left hand.

"Ugh." Was all he managed through his cracked lips. I'd have to take care of those poor lips later, they looked very sore. He turned his huge sunken eyes to mine, looking quite lost.

Next I reached behind him and undid the clasps on the restraints holding his wrists before turning my attention to the restraints on his ankles. Once he was untethered I stood back allowing him room to get up. I still had my gun trained on him - just in case. To my surprise he just lay there, he didn't seem to acknowledge that he was free. He just continued staring at me through those haunted eyes. I hated what this process was doing to him, but I just knew it was worth it in the long run. I was being cruel to be kind. "Come on David, time to get up, time to get clean."

He just lay there, almost in a stupor, making no attempt to move at all.

"Come on David, move it!"

No response.

I was hopping from one foot to the other. The smell of urine was getting to me. I wanted David clean and tethered up safe - in clean bedding whilst I got a bath myself. David wasn't the only one who'd got saturated in the night. "Stop messing around David. MOVE IT!"

Nothing.

He was really trying my temper now; I could feel my blood starting to boil. I didn't have time for this shit. Finally, I saw that I had no other alternative, so I removed the whip I brought with me from the wardrobe. As I approached the bed I expected some reaction, but no, nothing. I'm ashamed to say it, but I just snapped and whipped him across the chest as hard as I could, causing a welt of blood to well up through his skin. It snapped him out of his trance though. He screamed as I brought the whip down a second time, catching him across his arm.

And so it was in this fashion that I finally got him into the bathroom.

He sat blubbing on the toilet for around five minutes whilst I started his bath running. I made care to put plenty of bubble-bath in as I know he likes that. Once the bath was run I turned back to see him still crying on the toilet. I don't think he'd made any effort to urinate, and I found it most disagreeable to see him crying like that. He really needed toughing up.

I sat on the toilet lid while David bathed. He winced a bit when the hot water touched the fresh wounds my whip had made and I felt very sorry for using excessive force, but what choice did he give me, really?

"Why are you doing this to me?" He whispered.

"Because I love you."

He began crying again.

"Enough of that, wash your hair." I looked around the bathroom for his razor and shaving foam. After coming up empty I looked in the little mirrored cabinet above the sink. "Bingo." I pulled out the shaving foam and the straight razor. Ah now, I liked these. I used to shave my grandpa with one of these when I was younger. I was quite adept with one.

I put the gun down and knelt next to the bath, causing David to jump a little. His eyes flashed from mine to the razor in my hand. "It's okay," I told him softly, "I'm just going to shave you. Tilt your head back while I put the foam on."

He stared at me as if he didn't understand.

"Come on," I said, waving the razor, "*chop-chop*, I haven't got all day."

He slowly tipped his head back, keeping his eyes trained on mine.

"There we go." I rubbed the foam carefully across his lower face before raising the razor making him gasp a little. "It's okay, don't be such a wimp," I chuckled.

I was very careful as I dragged the razor up his throat and over his chin, I didn't want to hurt him. I looked at his poor sore lips with anxiety. I didn't like gagging him, but until his memory came back properly, what *could* I do.

What could I do? Mm. A thought had just occurred to me.

***

"Hello?" I fished my phone out of my handbag.

"It's me." Ruby said. "Are you busy?"

"A little, I'm just out in town doing a bit of shopping. Why, what's up?"

"Could we meet up? I'm in town anyway. Where are you?"

Shit, I couldn't think of a lie fast enough. "I'm…I'm…erm…I'm near the precinct."

"Great, I'll meet you in the coffee shop in twenty minutes. Bye."

She hung up before I had chance to get out of it. Shit! This I could do without. I put my phone back inside my handbag before looking down at my conspicuous carrier-bag. She'd wonder why I'd been in a pet store when she knew that I didn't have any pets.

I discarded the carrier-bag into the nearest bin and buried the shock-collar that I had purchased to the bottom of my handbag. There, at least the crazy bitch wouldn't see it and go asking stupid questions.

***

"So, what's so urgent?" I asked Ruby as I slid into the chair opposite her.

She looked uncomfortable and edgy. I wondered briefly if she was on drugs. She reached into her handbag and pulled out a folder. "I think you need to see this."

"What is it?" I couldn't see from this way around what the papers said.

"Look, don't judge me, but last night I ended up, well, back at *John's* house. Don't look at me like that!" She warned as she saw the scorn on my face. "Anyway, *afterwards* he got called away, but he said for me to take my time and have a shower if I wanted. He said just pop the key back through the letterbox after I'd locked up." She paused and took a sip of her cappuccino, blowing the foam out of the way. "You know what I'm like, I got a little…nosey. Had a bit of a look around the place. Before long I found myself in his little home-office, and what did I see sticking out of his open filing cabinet? A piece of paper with your name on it. So I got curious. Had a little look in the filing cabinet." She paused. "Paula, he's collecting a dossier on you. He has photo's, receipts, notes on your whereabouts. Seriously, the guy is stalking you."

I gulped. I took a moment to process the conclusion she'd come to. How would I play this? I didn't want to show too much of my hand to Ruby, I wasn't sure how much I could trust her.

"Say something." She said, sliding the file over to me.

"He's going to know you took this."

"He won't, this is photocopies that I took. I left the originals where I found them. He had a photocopier in his office so…voila'. So, what do you make of it? I think we should take it to the police."

"No!" I snapped before I could help myself. "No," I repeated a little more gently. "Just…Let me have a look at this stuff for a second, I'm a bit overwhelmed." I slid the folder over in front of me and started looking through the various papers. He'd been thorough that's for sure. There were copies of all the original articles from the newspapers at the time, plus a horrid photo from when I was processed at the police station. I gazed for a moment at my own dead-eyes staring back at me from the photo. I have no recollection of that photo being taken, but it's evident from the look on my face that I was in shock. The last page was a timetable of sorts, plotting out my every movement. I felt my face colour a little as I saw David's address popping up frequently - late at night from the various times I'd been watching his house from his neighbour's garden. I had no idea I'd been observed. After absorbing the last page I stuffed all of the papers back into the folder and slid them back over to Ruby.

"So?" She asked.

"Look, this doesn't really come as much of a surprise to me." I took a deep breath; I'd decided to be honest. "You know that lunch time when you set us up on a date?"

"Yes."

"He threatened me."

"He what?"

"He and his friends knew David. Remember I told you that some people didn't believe my story about David's abuse? Well, it turns out he was one of them. I didn't know that until the lunch date. I'd never met John before taking this job, and I didn't have a clue that he knew David. When he realised who I was - after googling me that day, he tipped his mates off and I got broken into that night and my house trashed."

Ruby stared at me open mouthed. "I can't believe it! Why didn't you tell me? Jesus Christ, to think *I* set you up with that psycho, to think I *slept* with that psycho!"

I just stared at her, I had nothing to contribute.

"You have to go to the police."

I couldn't, but she didn't know that, she wouldn't understand.

"You know that right?" She continued. "You can't just ignore this, Paula, he could really hurt you, I mean *really* hurt you."

"He won't."

"You don't know that."

"I do."

She sat back in her seat staring at me incredulously. "You're either really brave or really stupid."

"I'm neither. But I don't live at my house anymore I moved in with…Karl." For a moment I almost said David. I couldn't tell her who he really was because Ruby wouldn't understand.

"You moved in with him? Already? Jesus, you move fast girl!" She stared at me as though she was going to give me a round of applause. "Who are you Paula? You're full of surprises."

She had no idea.

"Well that does make me feel a little better," she continued, "knowing you have a man to protect you. Plus John and his cronies won't know where you are now. So that's a relief. I still think you ought to go to the police though. I thought he was stalking you at first when I saw that lot, not that he was harassing you, Christ, burgling you."

"It wasn't him that broke in. He warned me to get out before his mates came back and did something worse. To be honest I don't think it's him that's the problem, it's his mates. I think without their back up he wouldn't have said anything to me. I think he was just trying to impress his mates by 'outing' me."

She stared at me shaking her head. "It's not right. Why won't they get it that you were the victim? For Christ sake if there was any doubt about your innocence you'd be locked up right now, not sat in a coffee house with me drinking a cappuccino."

"Some people are just plain crazy."

***

"So what are you doing with your house then now you've moved in with lover-boy, giving it up?" Ruby asked after our third cappuccino.

"I'm paid up for another three months so I thought I'd keep it for now, it'll give me chance to decide what to do with my furniture."

"Why don't you sub-let it?"

"I hadn't really thought of that. It would be a bit short-term though wouldn't it. Who would want somewhere just for three months?"

"How about me?" She said, to my surprise.

"Why would you want it? You have a nice place."

"Yeah but it's a flat share, the rent's cheap but there's zero privacy. I wouldn't mind renting your place for a bit, as long as there's no bully-boys turning up that is."

I raised an eyebrow. "I can't guarantee that one bit."

"How about I tell John straight, tell him to stay the hell away from you and to tell his cronies that you've moved on?"

"I don't want to make waves. I just want to put everything behind me and move on. I'm even going to look for a new job."

"Stuff that, why should you lose your job? You haven't done anything wrong. I'm gonna have a word with John first thing Monday morning."

"I'm not sure I'm comfortable with that, let me think about it for a bit."

Ruby tends to be the sort of girl that gets what she wants, and by the end of our 'chat' she had persuaded me to give her my house keys.

"It's a right state." I warned her. "There's broken crockery and graffiti everywhere."

She scoffed at me. "I've got all weekend to clean up the mess and then I'll move in Monday night - after I've warned John to tell his mates to back off, that *I'm* gonna be living there now."

I was trying desperately to think if there was anything in the house that Ruby might find conspicuous, but no, I think I had everything related to David stored in our wardrobe at home.

Feeling apprehensive, I handed over my keys.

Chapter Sixteen

"I don't want it!" David cried petulantly as I
fixed the shock-collar to his throat. He tried to bite
me again which I really did *not* care for and told
him so.

"Stop whining David, this is for your own good,
can't you see? The tape and the ball-gag are making
you sore, with *this* I can go to work and know that
you're not screaming the place down, your skin
won't be sore and your jaw won't hurt. Now I've
set the shock level to ten, so it's going to really hurt
if you even utter a whisper. I'm turning it on now."

"But…" He didn't get the rest of his sentence
out as the shock kicked through his body.
Screaming only made the collar repeat another dose.
I hadn't wanted to tell David, but I'd gone on
YouTube earlier and learned how to up the power
on the collar. What it now delivered was a far cry
away from its intended output.

I felt bad for him watching him convulse on the
bed. He'd learned a hard lesson today. I used my
little remote to turn the collar off for a moment
while he got his composure back. "It's off now."

"Please," he whispered, "let me go? I can't do
this, I'm not David, my name is Karl, I know who
David was and I promise you I'm not him."

I ignored the nonsense he was spouting and
interrupted him. "Now I'm going to turn this back
on in five seconds. If you wish to speak, nod your
head and I'll turn the collar off while you speak.
Once you've finished speaking the collar will be
turned back on. Right, it's back on…now."

He started nodding his head quickly indicating
that we wished to speak. I denied his wish that time

because I knew it would just be the same old rubbish again. "I'll come back in an hour." I told him. I heard him start to utter something before the collar cut off his words. I didn't turn back to look at him, it hurt me too much.

I heard a very faint tapping coming from the airing cupboard as I passed, but it was very faint now, at least it looked like the problem was fixing itself.

After I'd had a cup of tea and got my pyjamas on, I brought down some of my personal effects from out of the wardrobe. It was a long time since I'd looked through some of the stuff in there, but I felt that now it was time to face up to my past, hopefully to learn from it. I pulled out the first restraining order I'd been given during courtship with David - before he died and came back. I smiled fondly at his signature on the piece of paper and after a moment held it to my chest. I pulled it back out in front of me and read it again with a smile. A thought suddenly occurred to me, once David could be trusted to be untethered, I'd have to make sure that his signature remained the same. He had such lovely cursive script.

Poor David had been in such denial about loving me in the beginning, it took me a little while to break through that armour of his, but I had, in the end, hadn't I? Although quite literally with a knife unfortunately. I sighed and shook the morbid memory from my brain. I'd do my meditation exercises later on and re-plot my thinking patterns. It was a trick I'd learned after my dad died when I was young. The pain when I lost him was so intense that I couldn't bare it. When I was fifteen my mum took me to see a psychiatrist to try and shake me out of my grief, but they were as good as useless. However, I met an interesting boy in the waiting room called Sid who taught me some skills about how to revamp my memories. I still remember that day as if it was yesterday and think of it - and him often….

***

October 2005

I sat in the waiting room staring at the floor and trying not to attract attention to myself. I didn't like coming to this place once a week to talk to someone who made me feel uncomfortable. The only good thing about it was that my mum wasn't allowed to come in with me, so at least I had a little peace from her breathing down my neck. She was in a café around the corner where she would wait until I joined her when my session was over.

I was staring down at my feet and imagining how nice it would be to give in to my urges and kick Dr Armand in the nuts instead of shaking his hand. The image of him doubled over in pain brought a little wicked smile to my face.

"What you in for?" A voice suddenly whispered from behind me. I turned and looked over my shoulder, startled. I hadn't heard anyone come into the waiting room, I thought I was alone. Now to my surprise there was a boy about my age sat behind me. He took in my startled expression with a grin.

"I…I…" I floundered for a moment at being put on the spot so bluntly. "I don't know. My mum thinks I'm depressed." I felt my cheeks flush a little.

I was used to people tip-toeing around me, not people asking direct questions.

"Well this place is hardly gonna cheer you up is it?" He grinned and leant back in his seat, pulling a pack of cigarettes out of his coat pocket. "Want one?" He offered.

"I don't smoke."

"So what do you do then? You can't be as boring as you look otherwise you wouldn't be here."

I bristled at being called boring. Who the hell did he think he was?

"I'll tell you what I do," I said indignantly, "I do whatever the hell I like!" I turned back around so that my back was to him. Now I'd given him a piece of my mind hopefully he'd go away and leave me alone.

"Oo touchy." I felt my heart sink as I heard him stand up and come around to my side of the seating area. Without asking, he plonked himself down next to me. "So what's your name anyway?"

"...Paula," I replied reluctantly.

"Well *princess* Paula, I'm Sid." From out of the corner of my eye I could see that he held his hand out for me to shake. I didn't mean to, but before I could think to stop myself I found my hand in his. I looked up into his mischievous smile as he suddenly pulled me to my feet. "Come on Paula, let's get the hell out of here."

***

"Where are we going?" I asked breathlessly as I hurried along behind him.

"We're nearly there." He called back. He started slowing down a little which allowed me to catch up to him. We'd been running through various streets and alleyways for the last ten minutes and I was now hopelessly lost. I just prayed that he'd get me back to the little café in time to meet my mum.

"Come on." He called, as he started pulling apart a hole in the wire fence in front of us.

"What's in there?" I asked, staring past him at an overgrown garden with some sort of building partially hidden at the back.

"It's my den. Come on, I've been coming here for years."

I was starting to get a bad feeling. I was suddenly feeling very silly for following this strange boy halfway across town and into some sort of derelict building. The only thing I knew about him was his name and that he was obviously having psychiatric help. If I wasn't careful I could be headline news tomorrow.

"It's okay Paula, trust me." He held his hand out to help me through the wire fence. I stared from his outstretched hand to his warm brown eyes that seemed amused by me and with a pounding heart I made my choice.

He led me around what looked like an old brick bomb-shelter, overgrown with climbers, nettles and brambles. There was a large security notice screwed to the brickwork with DANGER - KEEP OUT written across it. He ducked down and pulled a rotten board away revealing a small cramped entrance. "Hold on a sec." He ordered as he stepped inside. "I'm just gonna light the lamp because it's pretty dark in here."

I waited impatiently for a few moments before his head popped back out. "Come on then."

I climbed through the small entrance into - what seemed to me to be - an Aladdin's cave. The small shelter was like a hobbit home. There was a thick tatty Persian carpet underfoot, two small worn armchairs, a wall full of scruffy paperback books, plus a tiny round cast-iron stove which Sid was just starting to light. After he touched his match to the ready laid paper and sticks inside, the stove burst to life.

"Sit down if you like," he said pulling one of the tiny armchairs a little closer to the stove for me.

I sat down, quite bewildered at this new turn of events. "Do you live here?"

He put a large copper kettle on top of the stove to heat up before replying. "I do till I get found and dragged back to the academy again."

"Do you go to boarding school?"

"Not exactly."

"Where then?"

He sat down in the chair next to me, fidgeting with his hands for a moment before quietly replying, "Now don't go getting spooked or anything because deep down I'm a good kid, and I'm definitely not crazy or anything…but for the last year or so my parents had me put in a psychiatric hospital."

"Really? Why?"

He shrugged, "They think I'm a bad influence on my twin brother – that's what it comes down to really. Plus, me and other people just don't seem to …gel very well."

"Huh." I kind of knew what he meant. I didn't gel well with people either. "So you're a twin? Cool."

"Not cool. He's a stuttering snivelling little bastard. I hate him. I can't be around him without wanting to kick his teeth in. That's why they sent me away, to keep precious little Bobby safe."

I have no siblings so I didn't feel in any position to judge. But I think if I did have one I'd probably hate them too. I decided to open up a little. "I've been threatened with getting locked up too. These sessions I'm having with Dr Armand are supposed to be my last chance. But I hate that shit-head."

"Me too." He stirred the flames a little looking thoughtful. "So what happened to you to make you crazy."

I wasn't offended this time when he asked a personal question. I don't know why…but for some reason I felt that I could trust him. I think already there was some kind of unspoken bond between us. Was this what fate felt like? How could I only know him for five minutes yet feel completely comfortable with him? I took a deep breath and replied to his question. "My dad died a few years ago, in a fire. I was there and I saw him die, it was so awful that I can't get the image out of my head. It changed me, it's like something in me died and suddenly life doesn't feel real anymore. I feel like a ghost drifting through life, un-noticed and invisible." I found myself looking down at the Persian rug wondering how to articulate my meaning. "Like for example we're sat here chatting, but for all I know this could be a dream." I shook my head. "I can't always tell the difference anymore."

"Do you need to tell the difference?"

"What do you mean?

"Well which is better, the dream or the reality?"

"It depends I suppose. Sometimes the dreams are better, sometimes worse."

"Well can't you just stop trying to tell the difference and just choose the reality that you like the best?" He was looking at me earnestly, I don't think he was mocking me.

I was puzzled. "I don't understand."

"Okay, for example, your dad died, right?"

"Yes."

"So, what if you dream that he *didn't* die. Which reality would you prefer?"

"The one where he didn't die, obviously."

"There you go then. What if he really didn't die but you keep dreaming that he did? Isn't it better to have a horrible nightmare that he died but then wake up knowing that he didn't die."

"But he *did* die! I saw it happen!"

He shook his head gently. "It's just a matter of perspective." He reached over and tapped a finger to my temple softly. "It's all in there. Inside your head you have the memories of where he *did* die and the memories where he *didn't*. Both are memories that hold the same weight, they take up the same amount of storage in your head. Which memory would you prefer to keep?"

I stared at him, exploring his face. I hadn't realised just what a wise person I had come across. He made so much sense.

"It takes a bit of practice, self-discipline to chase the memories that you don't want away and to keep the memories that you prefer, but it gets easier the more you practice."

"So if I want then my dad didn't die?"

"Course he didn't die, that was just a bad dream."

"So where is my dad now then?"

"Where would you want him to be?"

I thought about it for a moment. "He's probably gone away on a business trip, that's why he isn't home at the moment. He'll probably be back next week and then I can tell him I love him and that I've had awful nightmares since he went away."

"Seems perfectly reasonable to me. Do you remember him saying goodbye to you and that he'd be back soon?"

I listened to Sid's words and I felt them starting to paint a picture in my head. It may have come from a few jumbled-up memories overlapping, but suddenly I was starting to see my dad with a suitcase in one hand and a plane ticket in the other. I watched him kiss me and my mum and tell us he'd be back before we knew it. The more I watched the scene in my head the more relieved I felt. My dad was alright. He was fine, he wasn't burned, he wasn't dead, he was just working away, he'd be back soon. I felt a tear slide down my cheek. I flung my arms around a startled Sid. "Thank you!" I cried against his chest for a moment before he pulled away laughing.

"See why would you need a therapist when you have me?"

"I thought he was dead."

"It's all a matter of perspective."

We sat for a while drinking the tea that Sid had made in the copper kettle. He was the first person that I ever felt such a connection with, he just *got* me.

As we were walking back to the café where I was due to meet my mother I asked Sid the question that had been bothering me. "Sid?"

"Hm?"

"If you escaped from the nut-house why were you in the psychiatrist's office? Surely if he saw you he'd send you straight back to that hell-hole?"

He stopped for a moment and turned to me smiling. "I'm not a patient of his anymore, but I remember that bastard well, he was the one that said I was dangerous and had me locked away. I went into the clinic hoping to brain the bastard over the head with something, but to my surprise I saw you sat in the waiting room and thought you looked interesting."

I blushed with pleasure. No one else ever found me interesting. "I'm gonna get in trouble when my mum finds out I ditched the session and ran off with you."

"So don't tell her."

"She'll find out. He'll ring her to find out why I didn't go." I looked up at the heavens for help. "I just have to hope he gets her answer machine, then I can delete the message."

"Well if you want to skive off next session, come and find me."

"I will."

He leaned into me for a moment making my breath catch in my throat as he softly kissed my cheek. He smelt like cigarettes and chewing gum which was now my new favourite smell. With a smile he turned around and vanished into the crowd.

I went back to his little den many times over the years but I never saw him again. Sometime later I came across an article in the paper that said he'd been killed in self-defence by his twin-brother after Sid burned down the family home with his family locked inside. All had escaped apart from his father who died in the blaze. Poor Sid, he gave me my dad back from the fire and then sacrificed his own. – At least that was what I dreamed happened. In reality I know that Sid is out there somewhere having a happy life and one day we'll sit in his little hobbit home, warming our hands on his stove and drinking tea from his copper kettle.

Chapter Seventeen

I had trouble sleeping. Usually with David laid beside me I would sleep like a baby, but not tonight, tonight sleep just wouldn't come. I had the feeling like I'd forgotten something, something important. I couldn't think what the hell it could be so I decided to get up and have a cup of tea. I'm normally more of a coffee drinker but after reminiscing about Sid I suddenly had a hankering for a cup of strong sweet tea.

I slid out of bed quietly so as not to wake David but as I made my way out of the bedroom I realised that his eyes were open. "Oh, you're awake too. Sorry, I hope I didn't keep you awake. I'm just getting up to make a cup of tea, do you want one?" I was awaiting his answer before I realised he couldn't answer as the shock-collar was still activated. "Sorry, I forgot about the collar. Just nod if you want a brew." I watched him for a moment but he did nothing but stare at me so I assumed that was a no. "I won't be long," I whispered as I closed the bedroom door behind me.

I flicked the landing light on as I was still a little unfamiliar with the stairs as they were quite steep. As the landing light came on I noticed a peculiar stain on the carpet in front of the airing cupboard. "What the…" It looked very dark. "Oh don't say the immersion's leaking," I moaned. I kneeled down for a closer look. The closer I got to the stain the more I noticed it smelt like stale urine. Ugh! That's obviously what the banging's been then, the bloody thing was definitely broken. I sighed and got to my feet, I'd have to ring a plumber tomorrow to come and repair it. I just hoped it wouldn't cost me dearly.

Once I made my cup of tea I got myself settled on the sofa. I'd pulled on David's dressing-gown as I liked feeling close to him. I pulled it around my shoulders a little tighter as it was quite chilly. I decided that I might as well update my journal while I waited for my tea to cool. I started keeping a diary the day I met Sid. Someone gave me a leather diary for Christmas but I'd never bothered with it. There was nothing in my life worth recording, until that day with Sid. Once my mum and I were home I'd rushed upstairs and grabbed the first piece of paper to hand to try and transcribe all the coping techniques that Sid had taught me. I hadn't wanted to forget a single thing. And so it happened, the first piece of paper to hand had been the little leather diary I'd been given for Christmas. Suddenly I had quite a lot to write down after all, and I've kept up to it ever since.

I chewed on my pen-nib as I pondered what to record - certainly not the shock-collar anyway, once that part of the training process was over with, that particular memory would be going in the bin along with the rest of the bad memories that I threw away. It wasn't healthy to clutter up your brain with rubbish. I decided to stop over-thinking it and just write from the heart.

EXHIBIT N

...My love, while you sleep upstairs in our bed, I sit here, only feet away from you sending you all of

*the love from my heart. Without you I was nothing
and without you I will be nothing, yet with you I am
everything, I am everything to you, I know it. Where
would you be without my love to keep you warm at
night? You'd be lonely, and alone my love. Together
we can bravely face the world and hold it in our
grasp. Together we are the world....*

    I put my pen down while I thought of a way to
end my memoir when my eyes suddenly fell on the
answer-machine in the corner, unplugged and with
its cord wrapped around itself. I got a little excited
as it dawned on me that I should record a new
greeting for us, after all David didn't live alone
anymore. We were a proper couple now and proper
couples have a joint answer-machine greeting don't
they. I should've thought of it as soon as I moved
in. This was an opportunity I had overlooked, which
was silly of me as every time I had visited the house
when David was out I had plugged this machine
back into the wall. How could he hear my messages
if his machine was unplugged? I unwrapped its cord
and plugged it back into the wall. As soon as the
machine had power the bulb started blinking on it. It
was silly of me I know, but I found myself shyly
wanted to hear my messages. I felt myself flush
with embarrassment as I pressed the button to hear
the messages.

    *David? It's me again, Paula. I don't think you
can have got my previous messages as you haven't
called me back. Or if you have and left it on my
machine then I won't have got it as it's…. it's not
working properly at the moment. So if you call and I
don't answer, keep trying. I'm in every day after*

6pm. Okay, I'll try calling you later. I love you David. Bye.

I almost leaped out of my skin with shock, after listening to my old message I realised suddenly what it was that I'd forgotten in my haste to leave my old house. My bloody answer machine! Ruby could've plugged it in and heard my messages! *Oh Jesus no. Please no!*

Calm down, I told myself as I started to hyperventilate. She said she wasn't moving in till after Monday once she was satisfied that John would put word about that I was no-longer living in that house. But she *did* say she was going to spend the weekend cleaning the place up, didn't she*? Please don't let her still be there,* I thought as I pulled my coat on over the top of my pyjamas. I wrestled my gloves out of my pockets and as I slammed the front door behind me I heard the beginning of a new message.

David? It's Paula again. Did you get my messages? I just wanted to tell you how much I love you….

***

I cursed myself for not keeping back a spare key. I hadn't had any intention of handing my keys over to Ruby, but she had been so insistent. I'm not used to standing up to bullies like her. It was looking like I'd have to try and start being a bit more assertive with people.

I got out of my car, still in my pyjamas – which fortunately were black so at least I didn't stand out to anyone watching -and slinked my way up the garden path. I had to keep reminding myself that this was still MY house. I felt like a common criminal peering into all the windows to try and spot an entry point. There was none, Ruby had secured the place up tightly. I made my way around to the back of the house as it looked like I'd have to smash a pane of glass in the back door to gain entry.

I'd never smashed a window before so I was quite nervous of it. I picked a loose brick up from the floor and held it up to the window. Several times I started to swing the brick- stopping just before it reached the glass. "Pull yourself together," I whispered to myself, noting the steam that came from my breath. It sure was a cold night. "This time," I told myself, and swung my arm back before hitting the brick against the glass as hard as I could. It shattered into a thousand pieces giving me clear access inside the door where I could turn the key into the open position. Thank god Ruby had left the key in the back door rather than taking it out. I was just turning around to discard my brick when to my horror a man came running out of the darkness at me. He grabbed me roughly by the left wrist snarling, "I've got you now, haven't I?"

I swung my arm back that still held the brick and hit him in the head as hard as I could. He let go of my hand and dropped to the ground with a whimper. I pulled my hood back which had slid over my eyes and tried to make out who it was that had attacked me. It was no good, it was just too dark. Whilst keeping my eyes trained on the figure on the floor, I reached through the broken door and turned the key, swinging the door open. I backed into the house and fumbled for the light-switch.

After a lot of scrabbling about I finally found it. As the light from the kitchen lit up the doorway I realised my mistake. The attacker was my next-door neighbour Barry.

"Oh god no!" I exclaimed as I knelt down beside him, leaning in a pool of blood in the process. "Ugh." He was either unconscious or dead. Either way he wasn't breathing. I had to do something. I ran through the kitchen and into the living room, picked up the phone and dialled 999.

"Which emergency service?" The polite voice asked at the other end of the phone.

"Ambulance. My neighbour's unconscious in my garden with a nasty head wound."

"Can you confirm your address?"

***

Once I'd given the lady on the phone the relevant information, she told me the ambulance was on its way and that the police were also coming as my neighbour had obviously been attacked by an intruder. She told me to leave the phone line open so that she could help me over the phone until the ambulance arrived. "But I have to go help him." I told her.

"That's fine," she said, "you go stay with him but leave this phone line open until the ambulance gets there. It's literally minutes away, hold tight."

I put the phone on the table and hurried back through to check on Barry. All this rushing about was making me hot, so I wriggled out of my gloves, coat and David's dressing-gown. After seeing all the blood on them I popped them into the open door of the washing machine as I passed.

Poor Barry, I thought as I looked down at him. He was only here protecting me and look what happened. He'd gone and got attacked by an intruder!

Chapter Eighteen

As I watched the covered stretcher take away Barry's body I felt quite sad. He was a nice man who had looked out for me. There hadn't been many men like that in my life before. I could hear his wife outside wailing as she was being taken away to be sedated. Poor woman.

I turned back to the policeman who had just sat down next to me. He asked, "So tell me again what happened here tonight? You'll have to come to the station tomorrow and give an official statement but if you could just give me a preliminary report now – I can start the ball rolling a lot faster. Catch the perpetrator as quickly as possible."

I nodded, shivering a little.

He took out his pad and his pen and gestured for me to start.

"I was asleep, then I woke up to the sound of breaking glass. I came downstairs to see what the noise was when I realised someone had broken in through the back door."

"And was the door actually open?" He asked, still scribbling away.

"Yes."

"So what did you do?"

"I put the light on."

"And then what?"

"Then I saw Barry laid bleeding outside the door."

"So what do you think happened Paula? Do you mind if I call you Paula?"

"Not at all, that's fine. I think…I think…"

He interrupted me. "Do you believe Mr Browne – Barry was attempting to gain entrance to your home?"

I shook my head.

"And what do you think happened?"

"I think he disturbed someone trying to break into my home. I think he was trying to help."

"At this stage, so do I." He admitted. "We found the murder weapon which seems to be a red house-brick. Forensics have taken it away, so hopefully there may be prints on it with a bit of luck." He paused looking down at his notes. "Did you see the perpetrator running away?"

"No."

"Did you hear anything? An engine starting up, a motorbike revving, anything at all?"

I shook my head truthfully.

He blew air out of his mouth despondently. "It's not a lot to go on until we get the report back from forensics. Can you think of anyone with any reason to try and gain entry to your property?"

I was unsure how to handle this question. Should I be truthful and admit to the hate campaign that I've been subjected to? Or should I keep my mouth shut and let them think it was a burglary gone wrong? If I was looked at too closely there was a chance they'd want to interview me at home again. I couldn't very well tell them that I don't live here, that would open up a whole kettle of fish with the whole intruder/breaking in thing. Plus, if I was honest and said I had now moved out – they might want to interview me at David's house, and should a meddlesome PC decide to have a nosey around the place they might not understand the relationship David and I have. So I decided on the latter option,

I would lie. Thank goodness Ruby had done such a good job at cleaning off all the awful graffiti from the walls.

"I can't think of anyone that would break in."

He flipped his notebook closed and got to his feet. "Righto, that'll be all for now then. I need you to come to the station – 9am to get your official statement. Okay?"

I nodded. "Yes, that's fine."

"Right well I'll be off as soon as forensics are finished. I'll just be sat in my car out the front - writing my notes up until they've finished. Do you want me to call someone to come and sit with you?"

I shook my head. "No, I'm fine."

***

It was around 6am before they finally left me in peace. I could still see a few neighbours peering out from behind their net curtains…but that was all. Other than that, I was back on my own again. I dropped down onto my sofa with a bump. What a night this had been! God only knew what Ruby would say when she arrived tonight to move in. She'd probably run for the hills if she knew what had happened here! I looked around me at the grey dust everywhere from the forensics team. I didn't see many fingerprints showing through it though, it seemed that Ruby had been very thorough with her cleaning. "What the hell do I do now then?" I wondered aloud. Apart from the grey dust on the surfaces the house did look pretty nice again, Ruby had obviously worked hard. It would be a shame to take this away from her, she was so looking forward to staying here for a while. Probably had half a mind to ask my landlord if she could renew the lease once my own had expired. I sighed. There was only one thing for it, I wouldn't tell her. I couldn't spoil her moving-in-day, could I? What sort of a friend would I be?

I set to work with the hoover and the bleach.

By the time I was done an hour later…you'd never know. Whilst I was waiting for my newly mopped kitchen floor to dry - I called an emergency glazing company to come straight out and repair the back door; and while I was waiting for *them* to arrive – I took down all the yellow police tape from around my boundary. *Now* Ruby would never know. After all, Barry's wife probably wouldn't be back to tell her about it for quite a while looking at the state of her as she was strapped to a stretcher screaming.

By the time the glazer had finished I had just enough time to get down to the police station to give my statement. It was lucky I hadn't taken all of my clothing with me when I'd moved out, I'm sure it would've looked very strange to the police if I had turned up in my blood-stained pyjamas.

Chapter Nineteen

As I left the police station I turned my phone back on. To my surprise, I had about fifteen missed calls from Ruby. Shit, did she know? Oh…I realised my stupid mistake and began dialling her number, I'd forgotten to call work and tell them I wouldn't be coming in. Stupid me! I'd been so busy trying to clear up one mess that I'd forgotten all about the other. Stupid!

She picked up straight away. "Where the hell are you? Are you okay?"

"I'm fine, I'm sorry I meant to ring in this morning and say I couldn't get in to work today but it slipped my mind, I'm sorry."

"So, where the hell have you been?"

"Oh, the police station."

"You got *arrested?"*

"No, burgled. Well, no not burgled exactly. Someone broke in, and my neighbour collared them before they could get in and then they…hit my neighbour over the head with a brick and killed him." Yes, I know this was a little misleading as she was going to assume that this happened at my *new* address, but I think it was for the best. Technically it was almost the truth.

Silence at the end of the phone.

"Hello? Ruby? Are you still there?"

"My god! I can't believe what I'm hearing! Are you okay? Are you hurt? Is Karl okay?"

"Who? Oh yes, he's fine, we're both fine. We didn't see anything; we just heard a noise and came running down the stairs to find the back door smashed through and my neighbour dead on the doorstep."

"That's so awful." I heard a little catch in her throat then. Once she was composed she continued, "It's them again isn't it. They've realised you've moved."

"No," I said firmly. "It was a genuine burglary gone wrong." I then added – thinking on my feet, "The police said there's been a spate of burglaries down our street for the last few weeks. They think it was just our turn unfortunately."

"It's just so awful, I can't believe it." She paused before adding, "If you want to change your mind about sub-letting your house to me I completely understand. I suppose your house will be technically a crime scene now won't it? Will you be allowed back inside for your clothes and things?"

"Oh no, nothing like that. It happened in the garden anyway. There's some yellow police tape out there cordoning off part of the garden, but that's all. Forensics have already been and done their thing, so…so everything's okay, as far as it goes. We don't have to move out or anything. So don't worry about my old house, move in whenever you like now."

"I can't believe how calm you sound. If that happened to me I'd be a snivelling wreck."

"I'm probably in shock," I lied.

"I'm not surprised, Jesus." She paused, "So are you sure I can move in tonight?"

"Positive."

"That's good. I had a word with John this morning and put him straight on everything. Told him I know all about their little hate campaign and that just because you won't go to the police doesn't mean I won't. I told him you'd moved now and that was gonna be my house, and if one of those crony's step one foot onto the property I'd chop their balls off." She then added, "I also made sure he knew that I've installed CCTV everywhere."

I felt my heart drop like a stone. "…You…you what?"

"Oh yeah, I wasn't taking any chances. I got a pretty good deal on it too. You can hardly see the cameras they're so tiny, but everything runs on wi-fi straight to my laptop. Any sign of any trouble and I can flick back through the footage and see what's been happening. Great eh?" She sighed, "It's just a shame that you didn't have cameras recording everything last night eh? Would've made the police's job a hell of a lot easier."

My throat was so tight I could barely utter a syllable. I cleared my throat. "So…where are the cameras exactly?" I was starting to feel faint.

"Oh, I've got one hidden in the roof of the front porch, one attached to the tree in the back garden facing the back door, and just in case some bastard actually gets inside – I've got one hidden in the light shade in the hallway."

Holy Shit! I was starting to hyperventilate.

"Paula? Are you still there?"

I had just arrived at the spot where my car was parked. I leant against my car for stability as I forced myself to reply. "Yes, sorry I'm still here, I was just…I was just unlocking my car."

"So what do you think about the cameras? Great idea wasn't it?"

"Yes…great. Really great. Look Ruby, I better go. There's a traffic warden snooping and my ticket's almost expired."

"Oh, you go then. But take care and look after yourself won't you. I'll see you soon. Oh and don't worry about work, I'll explain what happened and make sure they know you need a few days off."

"That's brilliant, thanks Ruby."

"No problem. Bye."

I hung up the phone, unlocked my car and collapsed into the driving seat. Jesus, this day was going from bad to worse! I just hope my David appreciated everything I was going through for him. I always told him that I would do anything for him, I just never thought that fate would decide to test me so rigorously.

I stuck my key in the ignition and started the car up. This new situation with Ruby was a problem. I'm sure that everything happened just the way that I told the police, my neighbour confronted a burglar and got a brick to the head in the process. I just think that some things are better out of sight and out of mind, and if Ruby starts dragging out CCTV - that could complicate things. At least she doesn't know the incident happened in *her* house not mine. She shouldn't have any reason to go playing-back footage from the last twenty-four hours, should she?

I put my car in gear, checked my mirrors and then set off home to tell David all about the night's events. Poor love must be wondering what happened to me. I was supposed to only pop downstairs to make a cup of tea. Look how that turned out!

Chapter Twenty

As I stepped into the house I noticed a peculiar odour. I wrinkled my nose up as it was very unpleasant. It smelt a little like a mouse had died somewhere or something. I hadn't noticed it the night before, but then again you don't always notice a smell until you go out and come back in again do you. But never mind the smell for now, I'd worry about that once I'd checked on David.

As I climbed the stairs I noticed that the smell was getting more pungent. When I got to the landing the smell got even worse. I looked at the stain on the carpet that I'd first spotted last night and realised the problem was probably that bloody immersion heater again. There was definitely something wrong with it. Today I would bite the bullet and call a plumber, this simply couldn't go on.

I entered our bedroom to find David just how I'd left him. I felt a little pull at my heart as I looked at him. Even after all this time he still makes me go a little weak at the knees. I could see from the way he was staring at me that he felt it too. He started nodding furiously at me and opening and closing his mouth.

"Hold on a minute," I told him. I looked around for the little bipper thing to turn the collar off. "Sorry, I won't be a minute, I think I've left the control downstairs." As I opened the bedroom door the awful smell hit me once again. "Ugh!" I pulled my jumper up over my nose and went over to the window and pulled it open as wide as I could, hopefully help to dissipate that awful stench. I stuck my head out there for a moment to try and cleanse my lungs and get my breath back. Once I felt better, I set off back down the stairs to look for the control for the collar.

I closed the living room door tight behind me to try and keep the smell out as it was starting to make me feel quite nauseous. "Where the hell did I put you?" I mumbled to myself as I started ransacking the room. I started lifting away cushions from the sofa in case it had dropped down the back. I stood back disappointed. All I'd found down the back of the couch were David's headphones. - Although that did make me smile when I thought back to the night I'd been in here when he was too distracted by his headphones to see me skulking around. I'd even gone up and laid in his bed. I'd gone home afterwards and put on my own headphones to try and put myself into his shoes for a while, although next-doors cat had scared me half to death. I smiled to myself, I didn't have to resort to silly games like that now, now he was mine, he loved me and I loved him, now if I could just find that bloody bipper thingy I could turn the collar off and he could tell me that he loved me.

I looked everywhere that I could think of but could not find that bloody remote for the life of me, so I decided to have a cup of coffee and try and mentally retrace my steps. It couldn't be far away.

While I was waiting for the kettle to boil I managed to get hold of a plumber who said he could probably fit me in sometime this evening -which was good. He said he'd ring me as soon as he was on his way, so at least that would give me time to get David sorted out. I'd decided that – as much as I didn't want to – I better give David something to knock him out. I didn't want the plumber hearing him and getting the wrong end of the stick. After all, he might not believe in reincarnation.

**

It was tricky trying to work out what David wanted, as obviously he couldn't speak without getting electrocuted. I had to resort to asking him question after question with him either nodding his head for yes or shaking it for no. It didn't help that he kept crying either. He'd gone and made his eyes all puffy. Eventually I worked out that he needed the toilet. After getting my gun ready I untethered him and stepped back to allow him to stand up and walk to the bathroom. To my surprise he suddenly turned around and tried to make a grab for my gun. I really wasn't expecting it as he was usually so submissive and he caught me completely off guard. Though his hands were still bound together, he was pulling at the barrel end with a fury I haven't seen in him before, if he wasn't careful he'd get shot trying to wrench it out of my hand. Then where would we be? I'd have to wait for him to come back in a different vessel all over again! I was trying to move my finger off the trigger when he suddenly lunged again. Before I knew it the gun went off. David screamed as the bullet grazed his shoulder causing the shock-collar to kick in and give him another dose of electricity. He landed back on the bed crying every time the collar shocked him. The more he cried the more he got shocked. It was a vicious cycle. I took advantage of the situation and quickly got the rest of the restraints back on him. The fight – it seemed – had gone out of him, for now. Also I noticed he had no more need to use the toilet.

Great, more work for me! I just hope he appreciated all I'm going through!

***

Luckily the bullet had gone straight through his shoulder and only gone through the fleshy bit just above his bicep. I wrapped a bandage around to stop the bleeding but decided that I'd wait until he was unconscious before I stitched him up. I didn't want him getting hurt - and that was sure to hurt.

Once he was bandaged up I traced the trajectory and found the bullet lodged in the wall. There was no way that bullet was coming out easily, it was buried too deep into the wall. I was just glad that the 'friend of a friend' who supplied the gun had also fitted it with a silencer. That little bit of extra precaution probably just saved David and I from some very awkward questions.

Stumbling into the bathroom I raided David's medicine cabinet in the hope that there could be something in there that I could use to safely render him unconscious while I stitched him up and got the plumber in-and-out with no awkward questions. The only thing that I could find that looked strong enough to knock him out was a bottle of *Temazepam* – which I deduced after reading the bottle were sleeping pills. Perfect.

I hurried back to the bedroom with my jumper pulled up over my nose. Once I was inside I shut the door tightly behind me and pulled my jumper clear of my face.

"Right David, we can either do this the easier way or the hard way."

He was snivelling by the look of it and facing as far away from me as he could get.

I offered my hand out. "Look, I've got some pain killers for you." It was a white lie I know – but needs must. He'd understand later.

He gave no acknowledgement of hearing me.

"David!" I said sternly. "You have to take these pills. They're good for you."

No response from the bed.

I sighed. There was nothing else for it. I climbed onto the urine-soaked sheet and straddled him. I had him pinned between my thighs and his hands were still bound to the headboard behind him. He was going nowhere and we both knew it.

"Now I'm going to pop the pills into your mouth and then hold the glass of water to your lips so that you can swallow them. Understand?"

He was still looking pointedly away. He was just as stubborn in this life as he was in the last.

I decided to join him in being stubborn. I got the first of the tablets between my thumb and forefinger and tried to post them through his lips. The stubborn so-and-so pursed his lips together as hard as he could to avoid taking them. "Just swallow them!" I hissed as he continued to wriggle and clamp his teeth shut. In desperation I nipped his nose closed with my left hand. He'd have to open his mouth sooner or later if he wanted to breath. After what seemed like an age he finally gasped, taking a breath. I took the opportunity to try and force the tablets in quickly before he clamped shut, but this was an error on my part as he used this opportunity to bite down on my finger, hard. I cried out as he clamped down harder and harder. "Let go! David! Let bloody…GO!" I took my free hand and jabbed his bullet wound which made him gasp out in pain and simultaneously get an electric shock. I also got shocked which jolted me much more than I had imagined. That modified collar could really deliver a whack. No wonder it'd kept him so quiet! I climbed off him, shakily and put my poor damaged finger in my mouth to sooth it. Gosh it hurt. I peered down at him feeling hurt, "You're just lucky that I can forgive you for what you've done to me."

He glared at me from the bed. I didn't like this darker side that I was seeing in him just of late.

I bent down and retrieved the bottle of pills from the floor with a frown. "Well David, you're taking these pills whether you like it or not. And there's more than one way to take a pill, if you won't take it orally then you've left me no choice but to give you them rectally."

He didn't look like he cared for it any more than I did, but at least that orifice couldn't bite me.

Chapter Twenty-One

It was done, the tablets were in and within a short time he was asleep. I had scrubbed my hands for all they were worth and then taken a shower too. I know that when you love someone you have to take care of them when they aren't in a position to do it themselves, but that didn't mean I had to like it.

Once I was sure that he was in a very deep sleep – and it was a deep sleep as I gave him a lot more than I was supposed to – I began cleaning and stitching up the bullet wound. I thought I did quite a good job of it really, nice neat stitching that should mean a cute little scar. No doubt it would be a talking point with our grandchildren one day when they ask where Grandpa got his scar. He'd laugh and agree with me that it was just a little war wound from the game of love – after all, *all's fair in love and war*, everybody says so.

Now that he was all patched up I began the task of cleaning him up and changing the sheets from when his bladder let go earlier. Now that he was unconscious he was much more amenable. I untethered him and rolled him over to the other side of the bed while I changed one side before rolling him back to change the other. He was very heavy and it wasn't easy, but I managed. I also removed his clothing while I gave him a wash. One thing that I found confusing though - on further examination - this time around David was circumcised. Did that mean he was Jewish? I wasn't aware that the Jewish faith involved reincarnation. I made a mental note to ask David about that once his memory was back.

I wrestled him into some clean pyjamas and then reattached the restraints. I stood back to look at my handiwork with pride. He looked so happy and comfortable lying there, all clean and fresh in his new pyjamas. I was starting to think he may be better if he was asleep all of the time.

I blew him a kiss and gathered up the dirty sheets and clothing and put them in the wash-basket. I was going to have a good clean around the place before the plumber turned up and then get all the washing and ironing done. *Oo I'm such a little housewife!*

I began with the hoovering as there was quite a bit of dust around the place. It's surprising how fast it creeps up on you. I thought I'd have a good proper go through, after all, as much as I love David, men just aren't as house proud as women.

I hummed to myself as I hoovered through from the kitchen to the living room. I decided to be really thorough and move the sofas in order to clean underneath them when I noticed a little bipper remote-thingy sticking out from underneath one of them.

"Oh at last!" I cried out in thanks. It had driven me around the twist trying to work out where it had got to. I picked it before getting a little puzzled. I turned it over in my hands, but it wasn't the remote for the collar after all. But it did have a large red button in the middle of it, so I pressed it. Instantly I started to hear what sounded like a smoke alarm going off from somewhere above me. After about ten seconds it stopped. I looked down at the device in my hand. "Surely that was a coincidence." I pressed the button again and sure enough I heard the alarm going off again. "Strange."

I followed the alarm all the way up the stairs, pressing the button again every time the sound stopped. Before long I'd traced the noise to the boiler cupboard. I stared at the door, puzzled and held my hand across my nose to keep the smell at bay. There was some sort of memory tickling away at the back of my brain but I just couldn't quite reach it.

I stopped trying to remember and began the arduous process of trying to get the door open. I needed to get the door open for the plumber anyway, so I might as well solve this little mystery at the same time.

Conveniently there was a hammer propped up next to the door, so I used this and slid the claw of the hammer between the crack in the door and the architrave. It took a lot of heaving and wiggling, and I cringed at the sound of the wood cracking a little, but eventually I started to feel the door freeing up a bit, though the smell coming from it was making me gag. I stopped briefly to cover my mouth and nose with my jumper before sticking the claw of my hammer back through the crack for one last heave. As it finally gave way I stumbled backwards as the door suddenly flew open – and something foul and heavy fell on me.

I screamed as the disgusting thing landed on me. Desperately trying to fight it off, I thrashed and thrashed until I got out from underneath it. I scrambled across the floor away from the thing, gazing at it in horror. What was going on? Why was there a dead body in the house? Who was it? What had David done?

***

I sat on the landing for what seemed like an age trying to understand what had happened. It took me a while, but eventually I plucked up the courage to approach the corpse to try and assess who it was. From my angle it was impossible to tell, all I could make out was a greasy head of brownish hair. I could tell that it was male, but that was about it. As I got a little closer I leaped out of my skin as I trod on the little remote I'd brought up with me, making the alarm scream out. It was much louder than before. After pressing it a second time I realised that the alarm must be in the corpse's pocket. Wait now, I thought, when I first got here David mentioned pressing an alarm that would alert security. I looked down at the corpse. Was this the creep that was following me? I threw him out the day I moved in with David. What the hell could he be doing back here, dead in my boiler cupboard?

There was no other explanation, David must've killed him.

I remembered waving my gun at him telling him he had to go. The next bit was a little hazy but I distinctly remember pushing him out through a doorway - and he was very much alive when I closed the door. I certainly didn't kill him. He must've come back. He must've come back and David must have realised what a threat he was, so he killed him.

It was the only reasonable explanation.

***

EXHIBIT O

...Oh my love what have you done? I know that you died for me to prove your love, but must you kill for me too?

Chapter Twenty-Two

What do I do now? I wondered. I could hardly leave the corpse rotting on the landing. No, I'd have to take care of this, bury it or something. I was tempted for a moment to heave it back into the boiler cupboard, nail the door shut and forget about it. But how could David and I live with that smell? Plus the flies would come soon wouldn't they? And then after the flies the maggots…Ugh. I shuddered at the thought. No, I'd have to find a way to dispose of it. It was the only way to keep David safe. Yes I know he'd done something stupid - but he did it for love, and so I'm going to protect him – for love.

First things first though, I better stop the plumber coming.

I tried and tried calling the plumber to cancel but he wasn't picking up his phone. It didn't even cut to an answer machine either, so I couldn't even leave a message to cancel. He had said earlier that he would ring when he was on his way, so hopefully I could cancel him then. But first things first, I had a body to dispose of.

***

I'd never had to dispose of a body before and I wish I'd had more time to think about how best to go about it. Obviously I didn't want to get caught, but how would I get it out of the house without being seen? It was a conundrum.

I explored my new home top-to-bottom and inside-out but found very little that could help me. The only thing I could find large enough to transport a body was one of the wheelie bins parked outside our front window. I pulled the curtains aside and looked out, I couldn't very well leave the body in a bin under my front window with people walking past it constantly. We didn't really have much of a front garden, more of a three-foot scrap of concrete under our front window. No that wouldn't do, which was a shame as a wheelie bin would be just the thing to move a heavy body. I was just starting to close the drapes when my eyes fell to the gated driveway of the house next-door. Although the house was joined on to ours -with it being an end-house it had a much bigger plot of land on it, and I knew to the far side of their house they had a neat little wheelie bin shed – set very far back from the road so no-one should smell anything conspicuous and perfect for storing a full wheelie bin until I could think what to do with its contents, after all, my neighbours were on holiday.

It was the best short-term solution I could come up with.

***

I felt quite nervous opening the driveway-gate of the house next-door and crunching my way up the gravel drive. I knew it was silly of me, the house was empty after all, plus surely, I should be more nervous when I return later with a *full* wheelie bin.

I made my way around the side and over to the large wooden bin-storage shed. As I hoped, it wasn't locked and fortunately the bin was empty. Good. I pulled it towards me and set off for home with it.

***

After a lot of trial and error I decided to lay the bin on its side at the bottom of the stairs with the lid open and facing the staircase. I then just had to drag the corpse down the stairs using the force of gravity and slide it into the bin. Should have been easy-peasy…but it wasn't.

I hadn't accounted for just how heavy the thing was and for how much bodily fluid the thing would leak everywhere. Honestly, these days I seemed to spend most of my time in the bath washing other people's bodily fluids off! Is this a common problem or is it just me?

Eventually I managed. I got hold of his feet and dragged him down – feet first to the bottom of the steps, without stepping into anything else unpleasant. I wedged the base of the bin up against the wall straight opposite my staircase so that I had something to shove against.

I was exhausted by the time I'd got most of his lower body in there. I was just hoping that as I raised the bin to an upright position – slowly, the body would slide down into it, enabling me to flip the lid over to close it up tight. I was lucky that either rigour mortice hadn't set in yet, or it had already gone past that stage. By the ripe smell, my guess would be the latter.

It worked out pretty well all things considered – although his body didn't slide very well, but then again, his hands were taped behind his back. I had a close look at his face before his limp body fell into the bin all the way. He had his mouth taped shut in the same fashion that I had taped it. David must've liked my style and copied when this creep came back knocking. I wondered how he died? I could see a lot of blood around his nose – and on closer inspection it looked like his nostrils were full of blood. Between the gagged mouth and blood-filled nostrils it looked like he'd suffocated. I hadn't hurt his face like that to cause such an extent of bleeding. Did David do it? A thought started to creep up into my consciousness but I was quick to slam the door on it, that wasn't a happy thought so it wasn't allowed to dwell in my brain. *Was the banging I was hearing this poor man beating his face against the wooden door trying to be heard?* I SAID THE THOUGHT WASN'T ALLOWED TO STAY IN MY BRAIN!

I was feeling much better once I'd heaved the wheelie bin back into an upright position, and as I hoped – the corpse slid down into the bin enough for me to flip the lid over and close it up. Good.

Now for a well-earned tea-break.

***

Once I'd had a rest and a cup of tea I felt much more able again. I would sleep tonight, that's for sure, I thought. The only things I had left to do was to take this bin back to the shed next-door until I could come up with something better, cancel the plumber when he rings up and then clean up this disgusting putrid house. I would be venturing out to hire a carpet cleaner later on, that was for sure. But first things first, get this damned corpse out of my house!

I went outside first to check that the coast was clear and that there were no passers-by. After a good look around up and down the road I was satisfied that I wouldn't be disturbed. I pulled the front door open all the way and began the process of trying to get the bin down the step without tipping the contents out. It was very heavy and not at all easy. I had to wiggle it a bit. I got first one wheel over the threshold – which made the bin lurch precariously to one side causing a lot of weight displacement before I managed to get the other wheel over too. The bin landed on both wheels with a heavy thud but mercifully didn't spill any of its contents. Thank goodness! Now I just had to wheel it around to the little bin shed next door and I was home-free.

The gravel was every bit as difficult as I expected it to be, but I persevered. I was about fifteen-feet up the driveway when suddenly the house's front door burst open – putting the fear of God in me. I'd been caught, I just knew it.

A pleasant looking young man of around eighteen or so came jogging over to me. "Caught you." He said laughing.

"What do you mean?" I spluttered out, panicking.

"Using my dad's bin while he's away." He gave a little laugh. "It's okay, I won't tell the old git, your secret's safe with me."

I was confused. He was staring at me with a grin on his face. Did he think I was just borrowing the bin for rubbish? He carried on staring at me, waiting for me to reply I suppose.

I found my voice. "Yeah, sorry, I'm a bit embarrassed, I thought the house was empty and I had too much rubbish to fit in my own bin. I'm really sorry."

He laughed good naturedly. "Think nothing of it. Like I say, I won't say anything to him. But could you do me a favour?"

I could hardly say no could I.

He continued without waiting for a response. "Could you keep the bin outside your house till it's been emptied? I don't know when collection day is, so I don't know if I'll be here or not. Plus with it being full, I can't leave it in the shed, it'll stink the place out if I do miss collection day."

My heart sank. But I couldn't think of anything to get me out of it. "Course, that's fine."

"Excellent," he grinned.

I started to pivot the bin around on its wheels when he suddenly said, "Here, let me."

Before I had chance to protest he'd taken the handle of the bin and was starting to heave the bin back across the gravel towards my house. I could barely breathe with fright.

"Jesus this thing's heavy!" He huffed, "What you got in here, a body?"

We both chuckled - him pleasantly, me on the verge of a breakdown.

We managed to heave the bin into position next to my own - just in front of my bay window.

"By, it whiffs a bit, doesn't it?" He commented as he stepped back, wiping his hands on his jeans.

"Yeah, I'll bleach it out before I bring it back." I really meant it.

With a wave, he left me to it. I went inside before I collapsed from the stress of it all.

***

I sat on my sofa trying to calm my nerves, but my eyes kept drifting to the green wheelie bin situated right in the front of my window. This was NOT good.

Chapter Twenty-Three

What the hell could I do now? Anybody walking past my house could reach over and open that bin lid if they wanted – and people sometimes did! I'd seem them walking past and dumping a crisp packet in or an empty beer can. Shit!

I'd have to open the bin and put rubbish on top of him, that way if anyone lifts the lid before I can think where to put him they'd just see rubbish. No passer-by was going to go sifting through a full bin, were they?

I got to my feet and headed out. I almost lost my nerve when an elderly couple suddenly ambled past me. I stepped back in the doorway for a second until they'd passed. After a careful glance up and down the street it looked as if the coast was clear. Good.

I crept over to the bins and lifted the lid on my own bin which had a few black bin-liners full of rubbish in it. Phew, at least I had something to work with. After another cautious look around I half lifted the lid on the bin containing the body. Gosh the stench was getting worse by the minute! I pulled the top bin-bag out of my bin and -despite my revulsion- put it on top of the corpse. I then ripped open the bin-liner making sure that its contents completely covered the corpse. It did look much better now and I was starting to relax a little. The only immediate problem that I had now was hiding the smell.

***

I ransacked the house looking for something smelly enough to cover the rancid odour of the corpse but didn't find anything that seemed strong enough. There were air-fresheners and things like that, but I didn't think that somehow they would cut the mustard.

In desperation I decided to raid David's tool shed, where to my delight – I found just the thing, creosote. Creosote stunk to high heavens didn't it. Perfect!

After carefully checking up and down the street, I lifted the bin lid and poured in five-litres of stinking creosote. It hid the smell beautifully – even if it did make my eyes water.

I closed the lid feeling much better about the whole thing.

***

The house took *some* cleaning! Well not cleaning as much as de-corpsing. After deciding that the landing and stair carpets could not be saved from the corpse juice, I had simply pulled them up, rolled them up and thrown them into the back garden where I would have a bonfire when I had the time. I then set about the place with a gallon of bleach and a ton of air freshener until all of the awful stench had gone and there was no trace of rotting body odour. I much preferred the smell of *Febreze.*

Next on my list was to wash the urine-soaked sheets that I had bundled into the wash-basket before I would take *another* shower to wash the latest addition of bodily fluids off me. It was starting to feel like groundhog-day, get showered, get covered in other peoples' bodily fluids, get showered again, get even more bodily fluids thrown at me. Do other people have days like this or is it just me?

I pulled the stinking sheets from the wash-basket and started to load the washer. As I did so, a memory came flooding back and my heart began to drop as I realised I'd made a dangerous oversight. I felt the colour pour from my face and down into my shaking hands. How could I have forgotten something so important? My blood-soaked coat and David's dressing-gown were still in Ruby's washer!

Oh shit!

How the hell would I explain that to her? Oh Christ, if she finds them first - she'll realise I've been in, and she might rewind her CCTV to see what I was up to, then she'd *really* see what I got up to. Bollocks!

Shit, shit, shit! How could I be so stupid?

I started to pick my car keys up before looking down at my corpse-covered jeans. God only knew what the boy next-door had thought of me! He didn't ask, but Ruby sure as hell would. There was nothing for it, I'd have to have a shower and get changed first, then charge round to Ruby's house to try and get my washing out of her washer before she saw it.

While I was waiting for the water to get hot I popped my head in to check on David. He looked so sweet lying there, I wished for nothing more than to climb in with him and rest my head on his chest. I would turn off his shock-collar for a while so that he could tell me how much he loves and appreciates me.

As my eyes drifted down his sleeping form I was horrified to see that he'd wet the bed again.

I could have cried. I didn't have time for this! I needed to get clean, get to Ruby's and get my washing back. Then I'd have to clean him up, remake the bed again and get showered…AGAIN!

There was nothing else for it, I'd have to buy him adult nappies.

***

I managed to get to Ruby's in good time, she wasn't home yet fortunately. I hadn't really thought through what I would do when I got there. I sat in my car outside her house wondering what to do next. I didn't have a key, and I couldn't break in thanks to Ruby's bloody CCTV. I was stumped. The only plan I could come up with was to wait here until Ruby got home, claim that I was traumatised from the previous evening's events and that I needed someone to 'talk to'. Hopefully while I was there Ruby might go to the toilet, or go off to get changed or something – giving me time to retrieve my blood-stained clothes from her washer.

It was the only thing I could come up with.

***

After half-an-hour or so I saw the number 10 bus go past. Ruby would be on that bus, but it didn't stop until it got to the very top of the street. She'd be here soon.

I checked my face in my rear-view mirror and practised what I considered a normal expression. I was looking pretty freaked out – even for me. I smoothed my still-damp hair and got out of the car, intending on walking up to catch Ruby on her way down.

Out of nowhere someone suddenly grabbed my arm. I almost swung a punch before I realised it was the middle-aged blonde lady who lived across the road.

"I'm so sorry, I didn't mean to make you jump!" She clutched a hand to her huge bosom. "I did call your name, but you looked miles away pet."

My heart was thudding ten to the dozen, she was just lucky I didn't have a brick in my hand.

"Are you okay love?" She asked kindly, "I saw on the dinnertime news what happened over here last night. I saw the sirens and the ambulance, but I didn't know what happened till I saw it on the news."

It was on the news? Shit! I should have known. Ruby wouldn't have seen it though; she was working today. Oh god, but what if it was on the six-o-clock news? Shit! If Ruby saw this house on the news she'd look back at her CCTV footage and see things that I didn't want her or the police to see. I didn't do anything wrong, but sometimes things could look worse than they really were, couldn't they?

I could feel the colour draining from my face bit-by-bit. Eventually I managed to whisper out a reply. "I'm okay. It was just…such a shock…"

"I bet it was my love."

"Hey Paula, what you doing here?"

My heart sank as I turned to see Ruby coming towards me. It couldn't happen like this. Ruby and this nosey cow couldn't collide. She'd drop me right in it!

My neighbour answered for me before I had a chance to utter a word.

"Hiya, are you a friend of Paula's?"

"Her best friend." She was looking puzzled at the woman who was placing her pudgy arm around me.

"Perfect timing then love. I think this one needs a friend right now, don't you love?" She said turning to me.

All I could do was return a weak smile. I was too paralysed to speak.

"You heard what happened?" She continued, "her poor neighbour getting murdered right on her doorstep?"

"Yes, I know." Ruby looked quite perturbed by the way this virtual stranger had me in an uncomfortable half-hug.

I finally managed to force a sentence out in a hope to end this awful potential disaster. "Actually Mrs…erm…if you don't mind I'd like a quiet word with my friend."

"Oh course pet." She let go of me a little. "I just saw you out of the window and wanted to check that you're alright."

"That's nice of you. Thank you," I added.

"My pleasure. If you need anything at all, I'm right across the street." She then turned to Ruby, "I hope that Paula's going to be staying with you till she feels better." She stared up at Ruby's new house. "I wouldn't want to stop in her house by myself after what happened in there." She then smiled at me before trotting across the road in her slippers back to her own house, to peep at me through her curtains – no doubt.

Chapter Twenty-Four

"She was a bit inappropriate wasn't she." Ruby whispered as we watched her disappear over the road.

I nodded, as my vocal chords seemed to be out-of-order with the flood of relief at having side-stepped another mess.

"How did she know about what happened?"

I shook my head. "I don't know."

She was still staring at me when I realised that I hadn't explained why I was there. "Oh, sorry to intrude, I was just feeling a bit freaked out and wondered if I could keep you company for a while? You know, take my mind off things."

"Course you can. You don't have to ask, that's what friends are for."

I followed after her as she headed up the path to the front door. Just as she was turning the key I spotted a stray piece of yellow police tape stuck under the privet hedge. While Ruby had her back to me I dove for it and quickly scrunched it up, discreetly sticking it in my back pocket just as she turned around holding the door open for me.

"Come on in." She said.

I followed after her feeling quite nervous. Had I missed anything when I was clearing up earlier? Would there be some bit of evidence left by the police that I hadn't spotted?

I hadn't realised that Ruby was staring at me until I looked up. She obviously saw me looking around the place carefully. "Oh, it looks very nice Ruby. You've done an amazing job on the place."

That seemed to placate her a bit as she visibly relaxed, shaking her winter coat off. "Yeah it took longer than I expected but at least all that awful graffiti's gone now. I had to paint over it in the end. At least there was some paint tins under the sink from when the place was decorated last. I only had to paint over the graffiti and not the whole house." She hung her coat up on the rack. "Would you mind putting the kettle on while I just pop up and get changed?"

Oh this was perfect, I thought. "Not at all. You go get changed, I'll make the tea. It's not like I don't know where everything is."

"True. Won't be a minute."

I watched her depart upstairs before descending on her washing machine like a vulture. I prised the door open quickly and pulled my clothing out onto the floor, cursing that I hadn't thought to bring a bag of some kind to put them in. I inwardly yelped as the blood from the clothes transferred to Ruby's nice clean floor. Shit, shit, shit! I hissed. I slammed the washer door closed and started across the kitchen with the bloody bundle in my arms when I heard Ruby suddenly call from the bottom of the stairs, "Paula, can I have two sugars in mine today? I could do with the sugar rush."

Oh god, I could tell by the sound of her voice that she was coming towards me. Oh GOD! I heard something from my bundle drop to the floor, I looked around me in a panic. I didn't have time to get back across the kitchen and get the washer open to stuff the clothes back in. I was running out of time. I quickly pulled the oven door down in front of me and bundled the clothes in quickly. I just got the oven door closed as she popped her head around the door. "Did you hear me about the sugar?"

"Yeah, I'll just be a tick."

"Great thanks." She let the door half close as she drifted off.

Phew that was close. Luckily she hadn't looked behind me and seen the blood below the washer. I grabbed a big chunk of kitchen roll of the countertop and a sponge off the sink and hastily cleaned up all trace of the blood. In doing so I found what had dropped from my bundle of clothes, the remote for the shock-collar! Thank goodness! I stuffed it in my pocket and then buried the kitchen roll at the bottom of the bin and clicked the kettle on. I was just about to transfer my bloody clothes from the oven back to the washer when Ruby came back in. "Do you want to have your dinner with me? I've brought a meat-pie home. It'll only take twenty minutes in the oven."

"NO!" I panicked as she rested her hand on the oven door handle. "I mean, no thank you. Let's…lets…get a take-a-way. My treat. It's your first night in your new home so we've got to celebrate with a take-a-way." I was thinking on my feet but she seemed to be buying it - the way she was starting to smile.

"Why not." She let go of the oven door handle and sauntered off back to the living-room.

Phew! I'd just have to wait for another opportunity to retrieve my clothes later. I looked down at my clothing to inspect if I had any blood on me. If I did then it wasn't obvious. It was just a good job I'd taken to wearing black lately. Another shower would still be in order though.

"Shall I put the news on?" Ruby called through as I was pouring the tea.

"NO!" I dropped the teaspoon with a clatter. The last thing I needed was Ruby to see *this* house on the news, it would raise far too many questions. "Let's watch a DVD."

"Okay."

***

Later on while Ruby was engrossed in *Bridget Jones* I managed to get back into the kitchen and was just looking around for a carrier bag to try and put my bloody bundle in when Ruby burst in on me again. She just would not leave me alone for five minutes!

I tried for hours to get an opportunity to retrieve my bundle but she just wouldn't give it to me. After a few hours of me lingering she began yawning and pointedly looking at her watch. It was obvious I had to leave empty handed.

With a stomach sick to its core and a dejected stride, I left Ruby's house and got into my car. As I closed my car door, Ruby closed her front door after giving me a little wave.

Good.

I crept out of the car and back up Ruby's path. It was very dark so I had to feel my way, but eventually my hands found the wire that I was looking for. Taking a pair of stolen scissors from out of my back pocket - I used then to cut straight through Ruby's ariel. There, now she couldn't watch the ten-o-clock news either.

Chapter Twenty-Five

I arrived home feeling sick and worn out. It was difficult to see my way inside - as in my haste to get to Ruby's I'd forgotten to leave any lights on. I got a strong whiff of creosote as I let myself in through the front door which was better than stinking corpse-smell I thought.

The only light I could see in the house was the blinking light of the answer-machine. I flicked the overhead light on and pressed the button to hear the message.

.... "Hi there, it's Mark the plumber here. Sorry I can't make it tonight, I have an emergency to see to, but I'll be at your house first thing in the morning to have a look at your immersion heater. Okay…thanks, bye." ...

Another thing I'd forgotten about.

When did life get so complicated? I didn't want much out of life, just someone to love and care for. Someone that would love me too and look out for me, worry about me and tell me everything's going to be alright. I wasn't greedy, I wasn't worried about big houses, huge salaries and flash cars. I just wanted a quiet life with the man I loved. Was that too much to ask for, really?

I made my way upstairs to check on David. Because he'd been unconscious for the day, he hadn't eaten or drunk anything at all. Hopefully - now I could turn off his collar, he'd be hungry enough to tell me his name and that he loved me.

I flicked the lamp on next to the bed and had a closer look at my love. He was still fast asleep bless him. I might not be able to resume his behavioural training tonight but at least while he was asleep it would be easy to clean him up, put on the incontinence pants that I bought on my way home and change the sheets.

It was nice to untether him for a while knowing that he was safe and wasn't going anywhere. Once I'd cleaned him up and wrestled him into his new clean pyjamas and sheets I lay beside him for a while. He was laid on his side with his injured shoulder facing upwards so as not to put too much pressure on it. I took advantage of this position and cuddled into him – spoon fashion. I reached back and grabbed his arm and draped it over me. Oh it just felt so good to held by him, to feel safe. This must be what heaven feels like, I thought. Although he was very cold, so I cuddled up to him extra tight to warm him up.

I hadn't intended to, but I fell into an exhausted slumber.

***

I awoke as the sunlight started creeping through the curtains the following morning. I couldn't believe that I'd slept right through like that. I was thrilled and horrified at the same time.

"David, are you awake?" I whispered as I lifted his arm gently off me. "David?" I shuffled out from under him. Bless him, he was still fast asleep. Never mind, let him sleep, I thought.

I stood watching him for a while, he looked so peaceful, it was such a shame I'd have to roll him onto his back and reattach the restraints. I'd been sloppy last night, anything could've happened, and then all my hard work would have been for nothing. I started to gently roll him over as suddenly a heard a very loud banging on the front door.

"Shit!" I hissed and ran over to the window to peak out of the curtains. Outside my house was a large white van. It was the plumber. "Oh shit! I whispered as I hurried to get dressed. I went back to the window and opened it and called through the gap, "I won't be a minute."

"Alright love," he called back.

Once I'd pulled my jumper over my head I slid my shoes on and hopped out of the bedroom quickly.

I stood for a moment facing the front door - with its intrusive silhouette behind it, and took a deep breath before pasting a fake smile to my face and opening the door. "Hi."

"Hiya love, I'm Mark the plumber. Sorry I couldn't get to you last night but I had an emergency came in. Some poor woman's stop tap burst so I ended up being stuck there for hours trying to get it sorted out."

I shook my head. "It's fine. I was actually trying to get in touch with you to cancel, but there was no answer on your phone."

His pleasant smile faltered slightly. "Oh, sorry about that. I had my phone on charge for a few hours yesterday. Is everything alright then? You got your immersion sorted out?"

"I... erm…yes. Actually, I had a man in there for quite a while and then when he left the problem was sorted."

"Oh." He looked a little dejected. "I'm afraid there's still gonna be a call out charge though."

"Why? You haven't even done anything?"

"But it's still taken a considerable amount of time for me to get here, and I've turned other jobs away."

"But I tried to cancel you…"

"If you'd cancelled before I got here then that would have been okay. Even if you'd left a message on my phone."

"I tried calling you several times but your phone just rang until it cut off, it never went to voice mail."

"I've had no complaints from anyone else," he countered, "I got all my other messages fine yesterday."

"Fine. I don't have time to stand here arguing all day." I raked my fingers through my unkempt hair. "What do I owe you?"

"It's eighty pounds call-out fee."

"Eighty quid? For doing nothing?"

He just looked at me and shrugged. He did look a little embarrassed though which I was glad about, he bloody should be embarrassed extorting money from a poor helpless woman.

"Hang on, I'll get my cheque book."

I left him on the doorstep while I went off to write a cheque. Under normal circumstances I would've stood and argued my point, but today I had far too much on my mind to mess about with trivial matters. I pulled my cheque book out of my bag and quickly wrote it out – leaving the name blank so that he could insert his own name. I didn't want to waste time running back out to ask him who to make it payable to. I tore the cheque off the stub and made my way back to give him it. Hopefully he'd then go away so that I could get back to business. I had a lot to do.

I pulled the door back open and offered him the cheque, which he gratefully accepted.

"Thanks love, and sorry for any misunderstandings."

"That's okay," I said grimacing.

He turned to leave before suddenly stopping and turning back to me. "Oh, while I was waiting I noticed the bin men are on their way down so I put your bins out for you. One of them weighed an absolute ton, what you got in there, a body?" He then grinned and half-waved, turning to leave.

I felt like I'd been kicked in the stomach. "You did what?" I stammered.

"Are you alright love? You look a bit peaky."

I looked up the street and saw the dustbin wagon just a little further up. God no!

I ignored the plumber and set off to retrieve the wheelie bin before the bin men could get to it.

"Hey, did I do wrong?" The plumber asked sounding puzzled. "I thought I was doing you a favour?"

He followed after me when I ignored him. I was panicking, which bin was which? Three bins were outside my curb, my own, the one with the body in – and a third which must belong to my neighbour on the other side, and I didn't have a clue which one the body was in. I tried to sniff it out via the copious amount of creosote I had poured in the one that contained the body, but it was no good, the bins were just too close together to differentiate by smell. I'd have to lift the lids.

"Sorry love, did I do wrong?" Mark asked, scaring the crap out of me.

"Yes," I snapped, "the heavy bin wasn't to go to the tip. It's my neighbours bin, they just…" *Come on brain, think!* "They just…left it outside my house because…because they're waiting for someone to collect it later." I stared at him, trying to gauge if he was buying it. He didn't look as though I'd just sold him a load of bullshit.

"Sorry about that, I thought I was doing you a favour." He looked contrite. "Which was your neighbours bin?"

"The heavy one."

To my horror he then grabbed the bin and started heaving it back into my garden, straining under the weight as he did so.

"It's okay, I'll get it." I tried to grab the bin handle but he shook his head."

"I've got it, it's fine. You can open the gate though."

I had no choice but to do as he ordered. I lifted up the catch and swung the small wrought-iron gate open – standing back out of the way to allow him room to get through.

"It's bloody heavy this thing is. What they got in here? Can't just be rubbish to be this heavy."

"I don't know. They never said. They went on holiday yesterday and asked if they could leave it with me until someone in a van came to collect it." I was thinking on my feet now that the panic was subsiding a little.

He heaved one wheel over a crack in the concrete, meaning to park it back under my window when the second wheel bounced over the concrete and sunk into a patch of mud causing the bin to tip over slightly at an angle. To my horror the lid swung back revealing the top of the garbage that I'd piled in there. My hands had already gone to my face in shock as I expected the corpse to come falling out.

"Shit!" The plumber exclaimed as the bin suddenly got harder for him to move now that one wheel had sunk into the mud – pitching the bin over at a precarious angle. "You're gonna have to help me with this lo…" He trailed off as he spotted something in the bin.

I didn't have to look into the bin to know that something must be exposed in there. The look on his face said everything. That was it, the game was up wasn't it. The police would come and arrest David for murder, and probably lock me up for disposing of it. Then we'd be apart again.

I couldn't do it, I couldn't lose him again, not now I'd found him. I'd simply have to find a way around this.

"What's wrong Mark?" I asked, deciding to play dumb.

He looked up at me and then back down into the bin before clearing his throat nervously. "There's a…there's a…" He cleared his throat again before whispering, "There's a body in the bin."

"What?" I whispered back trying my best to act shocked.

"Look," he said pointing down.

I made a show of peering in and looking shocked as I saw an ear peeping out from under a pile of used tea-bags. "My goodness!" I exclaimed putting my hand to my cheek in what I hoped looked like complete shock.

"What do we do?" He asked.

I knew what I wanted to do but I thought I better appear as though I wanted to do the right thing. "We better call the police."

He started patting at his coat pocket. "Shit. My phone must be in the van."

"Never mind, I'll ring from my landline."

He stood staring at me in shock, "I've never seen a dead body before."

Technically he'd only seen an ear but I thought it wasn't the time for nit-picking.

"Do you think it's a man or a woman?"

I shook my head. "Not a clue."

He was starting to freak out, I could tell. "Do you think they were murdered? Oh god they must've been." He was digging his finger-tips into his temples. "Who dies of natural causes and ends up in a wheelie bin. Bloody hell!" He paused for a moment panting, "Your neighbours haven't buggered off on holiday, they're on the run, that's what they're doing."

I wanted to get this sorted out before this went any further. "Let's go inside and call the police, okay?"

"Okay." He sniffed and wiped his nose on the back of his hand.

"Just a sec," I said, "can we just put the lid back on that and straighten it up so it doesn't fall over? It's just there's small children living next door and I don't want them seeing in that bin before the police take it away."

He stared at me for a moment, in shock I guess before nodding. "Yes, God yes, can't have kiddies seeing something like this. Okay, but can you give me a hand?"

Once the lid was back on he looked a little better. Once the bin was upright and not going to fall over – I felt better too.

"Come on then," I ordered, "Let's go call the police."

He nodded and followed me inside.

My heart was pounding as I led him inside, I wasn't entirely sure how things would go, but I was willing to try anything as long as it got David off the hook.

I made a show of picking up the landline after gesturing Mark to sit down. Instead of dialling 999 for emergency services I dialled 123 for the speaking clock. At least he would hear another voice on the other end of the phone, just hopefully not that they were telling me the time constantly. I then proceeded to have a five-minute conversation with the speaking clock – requesting that it sent someone out to my house as there appeared to have been a murder. I gave it my name and address before hanging up.

"What did they say?" Mark asked worriedly.

"They're sending someone straight round."

"I better wait here hadn't I?"

"Yes," I agreed sadly. "You're a witness. You can't leave."

Chapter Twenty-Six

Mark looked rather surprised at the gun I pulled on him a few minutes later.

"What the hell are you doing?" He lurched back stiffy into the sofa. "What's going on?"

By the look on his face he knew exactly what was going on.

"I don't want to hurt you," I explained as I held the gun pointed to his face. "I just need you out of the way for a while till I can think what to do."

He looked incredulously at me. "It was you, wasn't it? You killed that person in the bin?" He raised his hands up in defence and tried to take a step back.

I shook my head, "No. But that's not the point." Using my other hand I waved a reel of gaffer tape at him. "Now I need to tie you up and gag you. Do as I say and you won't get hurt, I promise."

"You're fucking nuts."

"No, just in love."

He glared at me as if I had two heads. Who was he to judge me? He'd never walked in my shoes.

"We can do this the easy way or the hard way. Easy way – turn around with your hands behind your back and everything will be fine. Fight me, or try *anything* and I *will* shoot you. Understood?"

He nodded very slowly. I could tell by his erratic breathing that he was terrified.

"Now stand up and turn around."

He did as he was bid, but was very reluctant to turn his back to me – with good reason as it happened, as once he had his back to me I struck him across the back of his head as hard as I could with the butt of my pistol. I knew there was no way

I could tape his hands together behind his back within only one hand. Knocking him out first was the only way to do it. He went down with a crash and although I hadn't managed to knock him out completely, he seemed stunned enough for me to quickly pounce. I dropped my gun and had his hands taped together behind his back before you could say *Jiminy Cricket*. Once his hands and feet were secure I stuffed a rag into his mouth and taped over it. At least he'd be quiet now.

I was just standing back and surveying my new little problem when I saw a dark shape suddenly pass by my front window. Was someone peeping in?

I looked back at my captive worryingly. "I'll be right back," I whispered before heading out into the hall and opening my front door. To my absolute horror I saw a bin man haul the first of three wheelie bins into the mechanism used for hauling them up and over into the lorry.

"NO!"

I ran as fast as I could to try and stop the inevitable happening. As I reached the wheelie bins I was panting, I placed both hands firmly on the bin that the bin man's dirty gloved hands were clutching.

"Stop!" I bellowed, as he started trying to move it.

"Watch your back there love," he chided.

I grabbed the bin from my side to stop him moving it.

"Hey," he said sounding surprised, "what do you think you're doing?"

"You can't take this bin. It's not for you."

"It was left out by *your* curb."

"I know, someone put it out by mistake. It's not for the tip."

"Isn't it? Oh. Right then." He shrugged indifferently. "This bin here is it? Because there were three of 'em."

I looked at the remaining two bins trying to gauge which one was the right one. Shit, I didn't know which one without looking inside them, and I really didn't want to do that now that the body was exposed. I tried to keep my voice level as I said, "It's the heaviest that I want."

He tilted forward the bin that I was holding easily and shook his head, "not this one then pet."

I turned and tried to lift the last bin and could barely tilt it as it was so heavy. It was that one. Thank goodness!

"Do you want a hand there?" He asked as I started trying my best to heave it back up my path.

"It's okay," I called back, "I've got it."

He shook his head at me, before turning his back and towing off the last remaining bin to the awaiting lorry.

After a lot of pushing and shoving I finally got it settled back under my window – with no dropping it this time. "Thank heavens for small mercies," I whispered to the bin and gave it a little pat. *That* little problem would have to wait there until it got dark, for now I had bigger problems.

***

"I said move it!"

The plumber glared at me from over his taped-up mouth. I'd left the tape on his legs just slack enough to allow him to shuffle, and where I wanted him to shuffle was upstairs so that I could lock him in the immersion cupboard until I could think what to do with him.

After all, it was empty now.

My new little lodger didn't seem inclined to obey my request though, and was stubbornly refusing to climb the stairs. I don't know what ridiculous excuse he was trying to convey to me through the tape as I was in far too much of a hurry to shut that shit down.

I know that I could've just shot him, but I'm no killer. I just don't have it in me to do something like that. I know my David snapped and killed the creepy man that was trying to split us up, but that must've been a crime of passion. I think that's allowed.

I looked at the whimpering wreck bound and gagged before me and sighed. In desperation, I brought out my whip.

"In there," I ordered. Gesturing behind him.

He shook his head again.

"Don't make me whip you again."

It took a few more strikes with the whip but finally I got him installed in the cupboard and able to slide the little bolt across locking him in. I looked at the slider bolt thoughtfully, *if he charged the door, would it hold?* My eyes fell to the hammer that I had used to pry the door open, perhaps David had been right about nailing the door shut.

***

I stood back, hammer in hand - to survey my handiwork feeling much happier. Now that little problem was dealt with - it was out of sight, out of mind.

I happily skipped off to see to my David.

**

It was a good job I went to check on David when I did as he was just starting to wake up. I got to work quickly and tethered him back up tight as he opened his eyes sleepily. He looked startled as I locked eyes with him. He must've been having a bad dream judging by the way he jumped.

"Morning sunshine."

He just stared at me without saying a word.

"It's okay my love, the collar's turned off," I whispered, stroking his hair softly.

He looked cautiously at me for a moment before clearing his throat a little. Testing if the collar was really turned off I think. Satisfied that I wasn't lying, he whispered, "water."

"Of course you can have some water…." I held the glass up waiting for him to finish my sentence like a good boy.

He sighed and screwed his face up as though he was going to cry again. He sniffed and stared pitifully at me through teary eyes before whimpering, "David."

"Good boy." I held the glass to his lips and let him take a good long drink. I stroked his arm softly. "If only you knew the trouble you've caused me. I know you were only looking out for us, but…oh my, there's been trouble David."

"Please let me go." He whispered.

"Oh David, don't spoil it. I'm not in the mood!" I held up the remote for the collar so that he could see me switch it back to ON.

Chapter Twenty-Seven

So I think it's fair to say that I wasn't having the best morning. The list of things to worry about was growing by the day. Why was life so complicated? All I wanted was for someone to love, and for that someone to love me back. Other people have that, don't I deserve that too? Why must things always be that much harder for me?

I had so many separate things to worry about that I decided that I better write a list so that I didn't forget anything important. Every time I started trying to fall asleep on a night some new thing that I'd forgotten would pop into my brain and hound me until the morning – when I'd probably forget about it all over again.

I've never had the best memory in the world, even since Sid taught me the memory game it hasn't improved that much. But, it seems especially bad when I'm under pressure, and by anyone's standards, I was definitely under a lot of pressure.

I took out my diary and turned to a new page before starting to write out the important things that I *mustn't* forget.

EXHIBIT P

1. Tea bags.
2. Milk.
3. Bin bags.
4. My blood-soaked clothes in Ruby's oven.
5. Ruby has my answer machine.
6. Plumber in the boiler cupboard.
7. Pasta sauce.

8.   Body in the wheelie bin.
9.   Corpse carpets dumped in the back garden.
10. Incontinence pants.
11. Bread.
12. Condoms.

I added the last item as an afterthought. We have to be sensible about these things, I'm not sure we're quite ready for children yet.

***

Several times throughout the morning I returned to my list to tick things off. But some things would take a bit more thinking about before they could be ticked off. For example, try as I might, I could not think how to get my blood-soaked clothes out of Ruby's oven easily. This and the body in the wheelie bin would have to be my priority for the day, and as I couldn't really go disposing of the body until nightfall, that bumped up my bloody-clothes in Ruby's oven to the top of the list. - Although on the matter of the body in the bin, thanks to the plumber who would be staying with us for a while, I could borrow his van to dispose of the body now couldn't I? I'm sure he wouldn't mind. After all, I am giving him a roof over his head. But as I said, that would have to wait until it was dark.

I'd been sitting contemplating how best to retrieve my things from Ruby's without drawing attention to myself when my mobile phone rang, startling me.

"Hello?"

"Paula White?" A male voice asked.

"Yes that's me."

"This is detective inspector Broadbent here. I wonder if I might pop round for a few minutes later on this afternoon and have a quick word?"

Shit, shit, shit, shit! I scowled at the phone in my hand and cringed as I said, "Sure, that's fine."

"Excellent, I just want to tie up a few loose ends."

I was starting to panic. "Do you think…do you think we could meet up in a café? Sorry to sound awkward but…I don't like being in the house now after…you know, what happened." I crossed my fingers and toes hoping he would take pity on me and believe my cock-and-bull story.

"Sorry, but I really need to visit the house again. I want to do one last walk through and then I'll take all the yellow tape down around your property."

Crap. But what option did I have but to agree? "Okay that's fine. What time were you thinking?"

"Let's see, is around three o'clock convenient?"

"Yes," I replied through gritted teeth.

"Excellent. See you a bit later on then. Thanks, bye."

He rang off without waiting for me to say 'bye' in return. I threw my mobile down onto the chair arm and sank back into my seat feeling nauseous. I just couldn't catch a break, could I?

***

I'd decided to look at the problem from a new angle. I thought to myself as I often did, *'what would Sid do?'* I tell you what Sid would do, he'd find an unorthodox solution, and that was what I must do. After all, if I played my cards right here I could kill three birds with one stone: - Show the copper around without incriminating myself, retrieve my bloody clothes from Ruby's oven, and collect my answer machine before Ruby plays the damn thing back and hears all my little secrets. It's enough that I have dirty laundry in her house without adding more to it!

The solution to all three problems was to regain entry to the house without giving Ruby any reason to go checking out her security footage. So, breaking in was out of the question. But without breaking in, how would I get inside?

***

"I don't know if I've called the right number here," I told the lady on the phone who had just answered brightly.

"This is N-Power emergency line," she answered, "do you have an emergency you wish to report?"

"Yes." I took a deep breath before belting out my rehearsed lie. "I'm on Chestnut Avenue, postcode JH12 0TE. There's a live electrical cable sticking out of the ground just outside my house. Could you turn the electricity off before someone has an accident?"

"Gosh that sounds dangerous, I'll have a team straight out to you. Whatever you do don't go anywhere near it and please try and keep anyone else away from it until the team gets there, alright?"

"Absolutely."

It can't have been more than fifteen minutes passed before I saw a van full of men emerge at the top of the street. After a few moments of fiddling away with a junction box I was pleased to see that the little red dot of my old neighbour's burglar alarm stopped blinking. The power had been turned off. Phew!

I didn't know how much time I had before the repair men realised they'd been duped and restored the power, so I set to work quickly while Ruby's CCTV was offline.

Unfortunately the police had removed my brick from the back garden so I had to make do with bashing the backdoor glass through with a plant pot - which wasn't ideal but it did the job. At least there was no neighbour next door to sneak up on me now.

It only took a few minutes and I was in.

The very first thing that I did on stepping into Ruby's kitchen was to call the emergency glazing company to come and repair the backdoor again, as I had to make sure the house was back in order before Ruby returned home from work. Luckily they said they could be there within the hour, so that was a weight off my shoulders. I looked at my watch, shit, time was ticking. The next priority had better be to put the yellow tape back-up around the back garden. I just hoped that the bin-men hadn't collected the rubbish from here yet as I had bundled the yellow cordon tape up and stuffed it in the bottom of the bin.

After a good rummage around in yet another wheelie bin – I found enough of the tape that wasn't too damaged and strung it up as tidily as I could. If the policeman commented on the state of it I'd have to say some of it blew down in the wind.

I'd barely finished when I spotted him trotting up the garden path. He was early.

"Hello again." He said, his jolly demeanour not fooling me one bit.

"Come in," I said, holding the door wide open.

"Sorry to intrude on you like this," he said, "I just wanted to do a quick follow up interview. Do you mind if we sit down?" He pointed towards the lounge.

I nodded and led the way through.

He sat down on the sofa looking stiff and awkward in his high visibility uniform and big black boots. I perched across from him on the arm of a chair feeling just as uncomfortable as he looked.

"So," he began, "can you think of anything else that happened the night your neighbour was killed? Any new detail that you may have remembered since you gave your statement?"

I shook my head. "No."

He looked disappointed at me, which quite unnerved me. He pulled out a folder from his bag and after wetting his finger began flicking through the pages. Finally he stopped on a page and folded it open. "When you were asked if you knew of any reason for anyone to try and harm or harass you – you said you couldn't think of a reason."

"That's right." I was feeling myself shrinking under his stern gaze.

"And you are the same Paula White who was harassed and hounded last year after you were acquitted of murdering your abusive boyfriend?"

I withered a little further and nodded.

"And did you not think that information would be extremely relevant to this situation?"

I shrugged. What could I say? *If in doubt, say nowt* -was my late grandpa's motto. What can I say, I paid attention! I sat looking at him without saying a word.

"Do you know who did this? Is that it? Have you been threatened?"

I shook my head. "No."

"So why didn't you mention any of this in your witness statement?"

"I didn't want to drag it all up again. It's too…painful." I paused, hoping I sounded sincere. "I didn't mean to deceive you in any way, I honestly don't believe the two things are connected at all. There haven't been any incidents against me for over a year. Plus I've moved twice since then and nobody bothered trying to find me."

"You're positive this wasn't a personal attack on you? Nobody's threatened you in anyway?"

"Not at all. I only didn't mention it because I didn't want to lead you down a false path. I'm sure it was just a case of a burglar getting disturbed and things going horribly wrong."

"I'm still going to have to look into it in light of what happened to you previously. I have names and addresses on file from when you reported incidents before and I'm going to have to look into each and every one." He paused, "This is murder Miss White. There will be no stone unturned."

Or brick – I almost said.

"Do you understand the severity of this?"

"I do."

"Now that the victim's wife has calmed down I've been able to get a statement from her that concurs with your version of events. She said her husband spotted someone dressed in black creeping around outside your house and so he went to investigate. She's assuming that what happened was a burglary gone wrong -which it might be, but it certainly doesn't rule out this being a planned personal attack on you."

I countered his argument. "If it was a planned attack on me then why did he resort to picking up a brick to hit my neighbour with? Wouldn't he have brought a weapon with him?"

I could see that he didn't care for my input, although I was quite impressed with my insight into the mind and actions of the perpetrator.

He got to his feet and made a point of staring down at the information in his folder before staring at me for a moment, slowly closing the file and sliding it back into his bag. I got his meaning loud and clear; he had his eye on me.

"Now if you'll excuse me, I'm going to take another look around the back and then I'll take down the police tape."

"Okay," I croaked out through my dry throat.

As he was headed out through the broken back-door he turned back to me, "I thought you would've had this door fixed by now. You can't be too careful, you especially."

"I'm on it," I whispered.

**

As detective dick-head was leaving, the glazer arrived. He looked a little baffled at me and the policeman. "Your door-window gone through again?" He exclaimed.

"Again?" The detective queried whilst holding my eye.

"Yep, second time I've done this door now." The poor cheerful window man said, having no idea he was dropping me further in it.

I stared back at the policeman and managed to squeak out, "it's not relevant and it's not connected. If you'll excuse me, I have things to do."

I then turned on my heels and led the glazer around the back to fix the door-window again. I took it as a good sign when detective dick-head got back in his car and left.

Phew!

Half-an-hour later and the door was good as new. Next on my list - I retrieved my answer-machine from where Ruby had hidden it in the cupboard under the stairs. At least she hadn't plugged it in. That would have made things extremely awkward.

The final thing to do before I left was to retrieve my blood-stained clothes from the oven, and then I could leave this house forever as far as I was concerned.

I open the oven door and felt my stomach drop as I saw the empty and newly cleaned oven.

I sat on the lino in shock. Ruby had found my bloodstained clothes! She'd found them. She must have. I didn't take them with me, did I?

I scratched my head trying to think. My memory was notoriously bad, but surely it was a stretch to think I could have done something and have *no* memory of it *at all*? I distinctly remembered putting them in the oven after retrieving them from the washing machine.

I didn't have time to think about it, I leaped to my feet as I heard a loud knock at the front door. "Shit." I whispered, grabbing the answer machine off the kitchen counter where I'd left it. I darted straight out of the back door, taking care to close it quickly and quietly.

I was shaking. That was *too* close.

I slipped away from Ruby's house quickly and got into my car. I noted as I left the street, the workmen looking annoyed from the side of the road as they turned the power back on, bringing the traffic-lights back to life.

Chapter Twenty-Eight

"Okay, next question." I held the water just out of reach of David's lips. "Who am I to you?"

His lips were starting to tremble again. David seemed so much more…damaged this time around. I wondered if that behaviour could be trained out of him too? I'd have to have another read through my animal training books later on. I had meant to re-read the chapter on clicker training anyway.

"Try again, who am I - to you?"

He took a snivelling breath. "You're my girlfriend."

"Excellent." I lifted the glass to his lips and let him take a long drink this time. "I'm so sorry that you're so confused David. I know things must seem scary to you, and I'm sorry for that. I wouldn't hurt you for the world…but you'll soon see, this was the only way." I rested the palm of my right hand against his pounding heart. "In there, deep down, you love me, you've just forgotten me."

He just gave a half nod, turning his blood-shot eyes as far from mine as he could.

"I love you so much, all I want is for you to be safe and happy."

He suddenly shot his gaze to mine. "You call this happy and safe? You've kidnapped me, starved me, abused me!" Spittle was starting to fly from his cracked lips with a fury that scared me. "You're a psycho, do you know that? Do you even fucking know that? I hate you. I hope you die and rot in hell. I hope…"

I'd heard enough of his bile and flicked the collar back to ON, silencing his venom and sending him into convulsions. I stared down at my hands, distraught at the hatred in his eyes. Why must he hurt me so? Why wouldn't he understand how much I love him?

The first David had doubts about us too, in the beginning. Although I soon turned that around. At first he thought I was amusing the way I used to follow him around, shyly watching him from the periphery of his life. I used to see him smile at me in a *bless her* sort of way. After a while though he seemed to get a little exasperated with me. I think it was something to do with his difficult upbringing or something. I got the impression that he was one of those people who didn't think that they deserved love. Things changed though after I made the brave step of moving in with him. He had more than a few doubts at first but once we'd been living together for a while he started to come around to my way of thinking. He even used to joke about it in the end, he said our love was something called Stockholm syndrome. I didn't know what that meant but it conjured up the image of a romantic city to me.

After a few months of gentle persuasion from me, I knew that David could now see what I saw, that we were soul mates. I think when he stabbed me he probably had the whole Romeo and Juliette thing in mind, two tragic lovers, too good for this world, better to die together than to live alone. I'm sure that was what he had in mind. That was why I had to stab him too. I didn't want to, but sometimes when you love someone so much you have to give in to their delusions, throw your lot in with theirs and see were the chips fall.

It seemed so cruel at first that I should live when my love had died. I didn't even have time to grieve properly as I suddenly had a murder charge to deal with. But I did my best, I knew my love wouldn't have wanted me to languish in a prison cell for the rest of my life and so I had to concoct a tale that sadly didn't show David in the best light. But I knew he would've understood. I couldn't really tell the truth to the jury, how could they understand the relationship that David and I had? Most people never get to experience that kind of intense love.

I was so lonely and miserable without him, until the day that I realised he had come back to me in a different guise. It made me completely reconsider my belief in reincarnation. I would have known David's soul anywhere.

I first recognised him when I passed him waiting outside of a shop. I almost flung my arms around him there and then but I didn't see a flicker of recognition in his eyes. I got up a little closer to him and breathed in his scent from behind. Oh it was him alight. It took every ounce of willpower in my body to stop me from reaching out and grabbing him. But I got the distinct impression that he wasn't ready, and to be honest, neither was I. This situation would need some thinking about.

And think - I did.

Now, staring down at him restrained and furious I was starting to think that I really had my work cut out this time around.

I left the bedroom with a heavy heart and decided to go drown my sorrows in the teapot. As I passed the boiler cupboard I heard that same annoying banging noise that's been driving me mad all week. If it carried on I'd have to call a plumber.

"So how does it work?" I asked Sid for the second time. We were having a second cup of tea in his hobbit home before I'd have to set off to meet my mum.

"Like I said, it's just a matter of perspective. I had this therapist once who had me write down everything that was bothering me, and then burn the pieces of paper. She said as the paper burned away, so would my worries." Sid was watching my reaction with amusement.

"Did it work?"

"As stupid is it sounds, it was a bit therapeutic."

"Do you still do it now?" I asked.

"Put it this way," he laughed, "what do you think keeps that stove burning?"

I smiled shyly.

"It doesn't have to be *exactly* like that, you can write stuff down and throw it off a cliff, stick it in a rocket and blast it to kingdom come. The point is, if you really commit the bad things in your life to paper, in the destruction of that paper, to a certain extent you can erase the bad memories of those things from your brain."

"Hm." I could sort of see what he was getting at.

"That, combined with altering your perspective to the way that you want to see things, it makes for a happier outlook. Look at me," he boasted proudly, "according to doctors I'm a fucking psychopath, yet to me I'm a happy healthy person with a slightly different perspective to most other people."

"So tell me again *exactly*, what should I do?"

He leaned towards me across the small footstool between us. He gently took the teacup from my hands and set it down on the floor before softly taking both of my hands in his.

"Paula, if you take every bad memory that you don't want, make a record of it, and then destroy it. Then make a new record with a better perspective. Ultimately, who's to say which perspective is true, the one you destroyed or the one you live with, I know which one I'd rather choose, don't you?"

I could feel the heat rushing to my face as he stared into my eyes, speaking so soft and gentle, making me feel that everything could be alright. I think I fell in love with him in that moment.

With a smile he let go of my hands and returned the teacup to me.

I could barely speak, this seemed like such a pivotal moment. I could feel that this meeting had been meant to be.

"It's getting late," he said regretfully. "I better return you."

I would've given anything to have stayed there with him in his little hobbit house, burning away our worries together to keep us warm.

I'm sure if Sid hadn't have died we would have ended up together somehow. I've tried many of times to change my perspective and have Sid still alive out there somewhere, but Sid was something so special that I couldn't seem to change a thing about him. He was a martyr and my saviour, and it seemed a saviour had to die whether you liked it or not.

I think that was what first attracted me to David, he looked very much like Sid and had the same calm demeanour. David even picked a second vessel that looked like Sid. Strange that.

It's just a shame that Sid wasn't reincarnated. I would have liked to see him again.

Chapter Thirty

My brain was feeling a little hazy again. I was too tired and had too much stress on my plate. It was so difficult to think when my brain was so foggy. That was one of the very brief occasions when I wished I was still taking some of the medication my doctor had insisted on. I usually hated them but they did help keep me calm when my brain overloaded. Never mind, I'd just have to wing it and manage.

I took out my diary and turned to the last page where I'd written my list. It felt nice to tick things off my list, it gave me a sense of accomplishment. After scrutinising it I realised that although I could now tick off most of it, I still had three things left to complete. Top of the list was the body in the wheelie bin. I screwed up my eyes, I was sure I had a plan of action for that earlier, what was it? Damn this brain fog!

I moved on to item two. Plumber in the boiler cupboard.

Shit! That's what the banging was. I'd forgotten about him again. After a moment a smile started to spread across my face as I had a eureka moment. I'd forgotten that I was going to use the plumber's van to get rid of the body wasn't I. Oh brilliant, gosh a van would make things much easier.

My smile slipped to a frown as I got towards the bottom of the list. "Oh shit!" I'd forgotten to get the bread.

***

I waited for cover of darkness to load the wheelie bin into the back of the plumber's van.

Fortunately for me, his van had a tail lift which made things much easier. I had been dreading trying to heave the bin into the back of the van by myself. I knew there was a good chance that I would drop it and I didn't think I could persuade the plumber to help me as he seemed pretty mad at me from the way he was banging his head against the door trying to break it down with his forehead. He'd have a nasty lump there tomorrow if he wasn't careful.

With relative ease I loaded the bin onto the tail lift of the van and pulled the bin into the back of it after clearing away a multitude of plumbing paraphernalia. What a simple easy job for a change!

I slid into the darkened cab of the van and looked about me to familiarise myself with the controls. I had never driven anything that big before and I was a little nervous. I also didn't know quite where I was going to dump the body yet, but I was hoping I'd get inspired once I was on the road.

"Righto then." I told the wheelie bin over my shoulder as I put the van in gear and set off slowly so as not to upset the bin.

***

I drove around for about an hour before deciding to dump the body in woodland. I had been hoping to find a lake or something along my travels, but the only body of water I came across was a reservoir and I didn't like the idea of dumping a dirty wheelie bin into the city's drinking water. It's just not very environmentally friendly is it?

I pulled the van over at the edge of a woodland thicket about twenty miles outside of town and turned my headlights off quickly. Although it was very dark, there was a full moon high above me making visibility quite good. I was very aware of how noisy the tail lift was though out here in the quiet of the woods. The hydraulics sounded deafening and it quite made me cringe. However, needs must. Once the bin was lowered to ground level I pulled it towards me carefully; it was so heavy I was paranoid about wobbling and spilling its contents.

I trekked for a few hundred yards or so deep into the woods, dragging my cargo cautiously and trying to avoid tree roots as much as possible. At the edge of a small clearing I admitted defeat and sat down onto a fallen tree to get my breath back. I was exhausted, the bin was so heavy and the ground was so uneven. I looked around me thinking that this would have to do, I couldn't go any further. I just had to hope that the body wouldn't be disturbed until the local animals and insects had done their job. I hadn't brought a spade or anything useful with me as I had expected to be dumping the body in water. I'd have to try and disguise it with leaves and moss I supposed.

I still had my hand resting on the wheelie bin handle as I sat there on the fallen tree, almost affectionately I stroked the side of it. "Oh if you only knew how much trouble you've caused me – creepy stalker man. Why did you have to interfere into something that didn't concern you?" I paused, "Well look where it got you!"

I looked about me noticing that when I spoke - steam poured from my lips into the cold night air. "I suppose as last resting places go this isn't too bad is it. It could be worse. My dad's buried in a….my dad's buried….my dad's…actually my dad's away on business at the moment but he could tell you a tale or two about bad resting places. There's quite a tradition of it in my family. My great-grandad is somewhere in an unmarked grave in France, poor sod. His wife was bombed in the second-world-war and her body was never identified. Then there was my cousin who drowned and was never found." I patted the bin, "trust me, there's worst ways I could have got rid of you. This isn't so bad."

Then why did it feel so wrong?

I sighed and got to my feet. "Come on then."

I decided to tip the bin over and lay the body out next to the fallen tree. I could then pile up the leaves and moss and things on top of it to hide it, hopefully for as long as possible. I took firm hold of it and began wobbling it from side to side until finally it leaned too far over and went crashing to the ground, spilling its contents out onto the woodland floor. I stood back in shock as I looked at the spilt contents of the bin. The body I had believed to be there was gone. I thought back in a panic. There had been three bins out on the front that day hadn't there? The first bin had gone into the wagon before I had chance to do anything, leaving me with one virtually empty bin, and one heavy one that I concluded must have contained the body. I was right about that though, it *had* contained a body, but not the one I expected.

I knelt down and looked at Ruby's ruined face hanging over the rim of the bin. In the moonlight her complexion looked beautiful, her expression so serene despite the fact that her left eye was hanging down her cheek.

I felt an annoying itch tickling away at the back of my brain. Did I know something about this?

I lay Ruby out beneath the tree and said a little prayer over her before gently laying the remaining leaves over her face, hiding her completely from view. I was sad, I had started to quite like Ruby. It had been quite a while since I'd had a proper friend and I would miss her.

I got to my feet and pulled the wheelie bin back upright ready to reload into the van when I noticed something else at the bottom of it. I pulled the now weightless bin around to the headlights of the van in order to get a better look at what was in the bottom. "My clothes!" I exclaimed, as I realised these were my blood covered clothes that I had lost in Ruby's oven. "Oh, thank goodness. And what's that?" I had to lean right down into the bin before my fingertips grazed the little black card that was stuck to the bottom of the bin. "Oh!" I exclaimed; it was the memory card from my answer machine. I slid it into my back pocket to examine later before throwing the bloody clothes back into the bin and closing the lid. Once the bin was loaded back into the van I set off for home, taking with me more questions than solutions.

***

I felt that little itch at the forefront of my brain, I'd come to recognise this little glitch - if you will, as a prompter to check my answer machine…that's where the answers could usually be found. I patted my breast pocket where I could feel the memory card from my answer machine protruding into my left breast. I put my hands back on the large heavy steering-wheel and drove on through the night feeling strangely calm. Suddenly I had that feeling of almost euphoria, as though things are finally going to get better. My David was starting to remember me more and more by the day, and now Ruby was out of the picture the chances of my being caught were diminishing. Any day now and David and I would have the life we always dreamed of.

I pulled up outside our house and turned the engine off, and just sat there in the dark quiet of the cab for a moment. My eyes had gradually adjusted to the dark and I felt oddly comfortable in the quiet of this large metal beast. As I looked around my eyes fell on the little catch of the dashboard and I grew brave and decided to have a little nosy. As I flipped the catch a small light came on illuminating the contents before me. I winced at the dirty cloth that fell out onto the floor before peering behind it at the rest of the contents. A boiler manual, various nuts and bolts and what looked to me like valves, and a little strip of blue pills. I picked them up with shaking hands at the thought of what they could be and held them up to the overhead light that I flicked on excitedly. I turned the strip over straining my eyes to read the writing. "Oh sweet lord thank you!" I whispered as my suspicions were confirmed. I held in my hand Viagra….and the means to make mine and David's union complete.

Chapter thirty-one

I let myself inside, hugging my bundle of blood-stained clothes to my belly and flicked the light on. Almost immediately I heard the boiler starting to make that awful noise again. I rolled my eyes and headed out of the backdoor and proceeded to dump the clothes onto my makeshift bonfire. I looked up at the moody sky in disappointment as it started to spot with rain. No fire tonight then, I mused as I shook my head and headed indoors.

Sitting down on the sofa I rubbed at my sore ankles. I couldn't wait for a nice soak in the bath and to cuddle up with my David. Technically we could do more than cuddle now thanks to the Viagra I had found in the van, but to be honest I wasn't really in the mood. I had tried to get David in the mood on more than one occasion, but I think he must have a problem in that department as no matter how I tried I just could not get him hard. I tried everything to get him interested but he'd just stare up at me looking frustrated and quietly pant as the vein in his neck strained against the pretty collar he wore. He'd be so excited when I told him I had a cure. No matter, I smiled. I had other things to do tonight anyway.

I pulled the memory card out of my pocket and crossed the room to David's answer machine where I slid my memory card into the aperture and pressed play. Immediately I heard my voice, squeaky and unearthly uncoiling from the machine like a nauseating serpent. I sat myself down on the sofa and prepared for the worst.

"My name is Paula White and this is my event that needs to be erased." I heard myself pause on

the machine. *"I locked a man away who I believe was trying to keep David and myself apart. I have locked him in a cupboard upstairs until I can make him go away. He makes a lot of noise that sets David on edge.... I can't have that."* I heard myself sigh deeply before continuing. *"Now I have committed my sin to the ether, I can erase this memory forever."*

My voice fell silent on the machine before I heard a beep. I found myself fixated on the stain on the carpet that I had trekked in from my muddy soles. Sid had told me about committing my sins and bad memories to a piece of paper which could be disposed of once its purpose was complete, but I had always preferred my answer machine. I could ring it up from anywhere and confess all my sins to it, erasing any unfortunate memories from my head at the same time. It was cathartic to me, I confess, get absolution and then move on free from the memory of my sin. Although now, it was necessary to hear those sins in order to fix this current problem. Once I had listened to this memory card I would know what I had done in the past week and therefore how to deal with the situation. With my work complete I could simply record my events again and delete them from my memory bank.

<u>EXHIBIT Q</u>

"My name is Paula White and this is my event that needs to be erased. Tonight I accidently...no, purposefully killed my friend Ruby. It wasn't my intention to harm her, but none the less she got

caught up in the crossfire of events that happened tonight. All I wished to do was to retrieve my blood-stained clothes from her oven and remove the memory card from my old answer machine.

After I left her house for the first time, I crept back up her garden path and cut through her tv ariel in an effort to stop her watching the news and seeing her house as the scene of a murder. As I was creeping away Ruby suddenly came wandering out of the back door with a laundry basket in her arms. By the look of it she'd remembered that she had left her washing out on the clothesline. I seized this as an opportunity to slide in through the back door whilst she had her back to me and steal my clothes from the jaws of her oven. Whilst I was sliding my bloodstained clothing under my coat, Ruby burst in and hit me over the head with a broom – mistaking me in the dark for an intruder. I hit her hard across the face with the large cast iron frying pan that was sitting in the hob next to me before I could stop myself. The first blow was just a reflex of defence, but in those few brief seconds I saw things with perfect clarity. Ruby knew there was something wrong, really wrong. So I silenced her in the only way I knew how. From violence comes peace, and peace is worth living and dying for. And so she died for my peace.

I managed to get Ruby's corpse into the boot of my car without being caught and took it home to dispose of in the only way I could understand for now...I put it in the empty wheelie bin next to the corpse bin. I would solve both problems at the same time.

I'm sorry that Ruby died, and I'm sorry that I killed her, but I had NO OTHER CHOICE. Now I *have committed my sin to the ether I can erase this memory forever."*

I heard the recording come to a stop and felt that all-consuming overwhelming sense of peace as I heard my sin and its absolution. For now I would keep it in my memory so that I could keep track of things, but then once I had cleaned up my mess and made David my own forever, then I would make another recording and forget these events once and for all.

I just needed to get a good night's sleep now and clear this brain fog, it was so hard to think clearly. What I needed was to lay next to my David, hold him tight and cry myself to sleep. No one understands my suffering like he does. He needs me close when I'm feeling this way, I hear his love pounding through his chest with every beat of his heart. His heart knows me, even if his mind is still confused. His heartbeat calls to mine and invites it to dance.

I pulled off my clothing and slid out of my underwear before slipping under the covers next to David. Nestling into the side of him I rested my cheek against his chest, feeling our hearts start to waltz together. This was what I needed; this was home.

Chapter Thirty-Two

I dreamed that Sid and I were sitting on a wall on the edge of a harbour looking out over the water. I turned to watch his face as he gazed out across the ocean, his hair blowing gently in the breeze made my heart flutter. He looked so at peaceful and at ease.

"What?" He asked smiling as he caught me staring.

"Nothing," I smiled shyly looking away.

"I love it here Paula, just watching the world go by, no people, no drama, and no noise but the sound of the ocean.....My mind's quiet here." He was smiling serenely at me. I blushed and looked away.

"Sid?"

"Mm?"

"Sid, do you think there's something wrong with me?"

He spun around and gave me a frown. "Paula, of course there's something wrong with you, that's what makes you so.... deliciously broken." He shuffled a little closer to me and took my hand gently as he stared softly at me. "Broken people are made up of millions of tiny fragmented pieces, like a jigsaw if you like, except there's no picture on the box to work out where the pieces should all go. That means we can take those broken pieces and rebuild ourselves how we want to be, not how we came out of the factory. You *were* a broken thing Paula, but now I'm happy to say, you are my masterpiece." He slung his arm around my shoulder and pulled me close before returning his gaze to the ocean.

I enjoyed the feeling of his arm draped around my shoulder and snuggled in closer smiling to myself. It was very peaceful here. I let my gaze wander from the ocean for a moment to the beach below us and frowned as I noticed a litter of white wooden crosses impaled across the sand. I leaned forward, squinting for a better look. "Sid, what are all those white crosses?"

He didn't shift his eyes from the ocean as he muttered softly, "collateral damage."

*****

I awoke from my dream with a start and for a brief moment was confused as to where I was. "Sid?" I called out. I paused a moment trying to collect my thoughts. "Oh. David?" I heard a soft murmur next to me in the dark which I realised straight away was my David. I was okay, I was home. It was just the dream confusing me for a moment. I reached out and turned the lamp on next to me. The sudden burst of light seemed glaring and made me squint. I yawned and looked across at David. If I didn't know better I'd say he was crying again. I find crying in men very unattractive at the best of times, so I was annoyed at his crocodile tears right now. What did he have to snivel about? He got to lay in bed all day whilst I - his virtual slave- waited on him hand and foot! If anyone deserved a good cry, it's me!

"You're so ungrateful," I told him. He looked me dead in the eyes with a look that I just couldn't read. I stared for a little while wondering if I should turn the collar off and let him speak. But was there really any point, it would just be something trivial -

as is his way lately. He was so difficult to work out this time around, I thought we'd be much further along the process by now. I stared at him intently trying to work out what that look was. It was such an intense look. "Wait…" Could he finally be? "David, are you…. are you horny?" His eyes flared a little and despite him shaking his head coyly I knew that dilated pupils were a sign of sexual arousal. It was the only explanation I could come up with. "Mm." I whispered as I pulled myself up and over until I was straddling him. Naked, and staring down at his greedy eyes, I slowly rocked back and forth grinding myself against him waiting to feel him getting hard beneath me. After a few minutes of nothing happening I slid over and pulled the blanket down to free us both a little. I didn't find the sight of his nappy very alluring, but it was so well padded that it would be difficult to feel anything hard under there. As provocatively as I could I pealed back the Velcro tabs to reveal his hard member, only to find a flaccid stinking worm that let loose and pissed in my face.

FUCK MY LIFE.

***

I was starting to get used to these middle of the night baths now. It was an endless cycle of other people's juices polluting me – and not in the manner I had hoped for.

I was under so much pressure spinning all of these plates, I hadn't even had time to go to work – or even call in sick for that matter. I think it was fair to say I was probably sacked on top of everything else that was going wrong. I would have to write another list to help me figure out what my priorities were. Top of the list was the plumber in the cupboard. He'd been quiet for hours but I knew that wouldn't last long. He'd soon be throwing himself at the door again deliberately annoying in the beat. The rhythm he made earlier as he threw himself at the door was to the beat of *Billy Jean, by Michael Jackson.* I'd found myself standing outside the door, puzzled at first trying to work out what the sound reminded me of. As it dawned on me he was beating out Billy Jean I shrugged and began singing along with him. I don't know if I sang it wrong or off key but he soon stopped. If the guy was musical maybe he was in a band or something?

Second on the list was the corpse carpets which would soon start attracting attention if I wasn't careful. If I can't get the weather for a bonfire then they might have to be dumped. In fact whilst I had the plumbers van I could maybe even do a tip run? I could do with getting rid of a lot of David's furniture anyway, mine – what was left of it, was much nicer.

Third on the list was to do some more research onto how to help David remember me.

I lay back letting the hot water flood over me, relishing in the sensation of warmth and comfort. I closed my eyes and started drifting for a moment before a sudden pounding from the boiler cupboard disturbed my peace. I cocked my head to one side and listened intently. He was pounding out something softer this time. It suited my mood. I smiled as I realised what it was, *Elvis – Heart break hotel.* I nodded approvingly at his choice and began to sing along softly, *"I've been so lonely...Been so lonely, I could die."*

Chapter thirty-three

I awoke late the following morning, only waking due to the doorbell ringing continuously. "Oh God what now?" I grumbled staggering out of bed and slipping my robe on. "Hang on, hang on!" I shouted in a bid to halt the noise from the door. I bundled past the equally noisy boiler cupboard door and made my way down the stairs. I could just make out a hulking great shape through the glass but no real details.

I flung open the door aggressively to find Detective Dickhead back upon my doorstep.

"Well this is a turnup for the book!" He was staring at me in a rather odd fashion. "I've been looking for you Paula." I didn't like the way he was stood assessing me for what seemed like an age. He finally cleared his throat and found his voice. "I'd like to come inside and talk to you!" It was clearly not a question.

I held the door open wide without saying a word and let him breeze past me into the living room. He sat down without being offered first, I found that quite rude and presumptuous.

"So Paula, what are you doing at this address?"

"I'm staying with my boyfriend."

He gave me a long judgemental look. "Is there anything you want to tell me?"

I shook my head feeling suddenly afraid.

"Well, this is an odd situation, I had a missing person report come through that a man called Mark Brown is missing. Tell me now, do you know anything about that Paula?"

I shook my head. "Name doesn't ring a bell."

"Oh really?" He raised his hand up to scratch his chin. "Well that is very odd. Mark is a local plumber and his last-known whereabouts was this address."

"I don't know anything about that. I did call a plumber but then I didn't need one anymore so I called him and cancelled."

"Paula, his van is sitting outside *this* house. The van has a tracker on it, I've just had it tracked to *this very house*. What do you have to say?"

I thought for a moment, "Would you like a cup of tea?"

"PAULA!" He shouted, "Where is Mark Brown? And for that matter where is Ruby Richardson? I've been trying to get in touch with you about her disappearance all week!"

I couldn't think. I was just very aware of the beat of the song starting to pound out from the cupboard upstairs. *Please not now!*

"What's that noise?"

"Mm?" I didn't know how to respond.

"That pounding upstairs?"

"I don't hear anyth…Oh, the boiler you mean? Yes it is quite loud. That was why I was looking for a plumber. Though I didn't actually get one." I hastily added.

Before I could think what was happening, Detective dickhead was on his feet and heading up the stairs at full pelt.

"Shit!" I cursed running after him. "Wait!" I looked around me for a weapon, my eyes falling to the pistol I had left sticking out down the side of my chair. Snatching it up, I chased the detective up the stairs. I leaped to the top of the stairs to find the landing empty even though the pounding was louder than ever. There was only one place he could be. I burst through my bedroom door to find the detective untethering David. "Stop right there." I ordered holding my pistol high.

The detective stopped what he was doing and backed away a step, raising his hands slowly above his head. "Now calm down Paula, don't do anything hasty."

David started coughing loudly and I realised that the detective had taken his collar off. David must have heard the cop coming up the stairs and shouted for help before getting shocked into silence once again. I stood staring at them, from one to the other.

"What now then Paula?" The detective asked. "Backup will be here very quickly. Put down the gun and let's talk. You don't want to get in any more trouble. Just put down the gun and tell me what's going on here."

"Shush." I told him. "I just need to think." It couldn't end like this. I was so close to tying up all the loose ends and actually been able to breathe easy again. I paced up and down behind David, trying to gather my senses and find a way out of this. "Okay," I said as I thought of something. "I'm sorry officer," I lowered my gun, "it's not what it looks like. Me and David were just playing a…a…. a role-playing game and I guess I just got caught up in the moment. I'm so sorry to scare you."

He stared back darkly. "Put the gun down."

"It's not real."

"So put it down then."

"I…it's…look…."

"Please help me!" David croaked from the bed.

"Oh don't start now David, I'm kind of in the middle of something here."

"I'm not David," he sobbed. "My name is Karl Boon and I've been kidnapped!" He seemed to be in a sudden rage and started thrashing about and fighting his remaining restraint that was holding his right arm down. Although his left arm had already been freed, the damage the bullet had made to his left shoulder seemed to be impairing his ability to move his arm across to undo his remaining restraint. He was thrashing and sweating with his teeth bared like an animal. I think my heart broke right there and then as I watched him. After everything I had done for him. Every awful thing I'd had to do to keep him safe. It hit me like a shot through the heart. David didn't love me.

I must've been distracted for a moment as I didn't see the blow to my head coming until the detective had already taken me down. I lost both my will to live and my grip on the gun and crashed down against the chest of drawers.

"Paula White, you have the right to remain silent…Anything you do say, can and will be used against you in a court of law…."

I sat on the floor with my hands on top of my head as I was read my rights. I didn't struggle as the handcuffs went on; I just couldn't find the enthusiasm to fight back.

It was over.

I watched in silence as David was freed from his restraints. He was very shaky on his feet as he limped away from the bed - still crying, I noted. I don't think I or the detective suspected that David - once free would pick up the gun from where I dropped it and shoot me in the chest with it. It didn't hurt, but the force blew me back against the wall before I slid down into a pool of blood on the floor. I was winded and I couldn't catch my breath, but the blood was so fascinating as it raced to leave my body. I could feel my heart pounding, pumping the blood out faster. My hands were shaking as I reached out, still-handcuffed - to draw a heart in the blood.

"Love hurts." I whispered as I slipped away into a dark fog.

Chapter thirty-four

I could hear voices for a while drifting into my dreams. I tried to answer them, to call out, but I couldn't find the strength to make my lips move. I was scared as I heard fragmented sentences that made no sense, such as – "Probably better this one doesn't make it." And, "You know who she is don't you?"

I don't know how long I drifted like this, half-dead and half-dreaming, but gradually my dreams started to fall away and I became more aware of my surroundings. I felt…cold.

When I finally managed to open my eyes I was almost blinded by the pinprick of light that gradually grew and grew until it became daylight, and I was back once more to witness the dawn light shining through my barred window.

"Hello?" I croaked through cracked lips as I tried to raise myself up in the bed. I couldn't seem to move my arms from the bed. I tried sitting up again – starting to panic. It was no use, I couldn't move.

"Whoa there," Detective Broadbent ordered from the chair next to my hospital bed. "Steady on or you'll do yourself some damage. Hold on while I get a nurse."

I stared from one manacled wrist to the other. The handcuffs holding my wrists to the bed seemed unnecessarily tight. My brain was foggy and I was struggling to think coherently, though through the fog I was realising that my chest hurt… A LOT. "Ow." I cried out to myself as the pain level started creeping up. I looked down at my bandaged chest and saw blood starting to seep its way through.

"Help me!" I cried, panicking and trying desperately to free myself. "PLEASE! PLEASE WILL SOMEONE LET ME OUT!! PLEASE DON'T LEAVE ME LIKE THIS!" I yanked at my restraints. "YOU CAN'T LEAVE ME TIED UP LIKE THIS!" I started to cry and scream as the nurse came running in with a big syringe of sleepy bye-byes. I cried and fought with every fibre of my being until I felt myself drift away into back into the fog where I dreamed Sid was waiting for me in our little hobbit home.

The End

Epilogue

21/06/20 Daily metro news

29-year-old Paula White was yesterday found guilty of triple murder, kidnapping, and attempted murder.

White, pleaded not guilty on the grounds of diminished responsibility, but the jury disagreed and found her guilty on all counts. She begins her 45-year sentence from the comfort of Broadmoor psychiatric hospital after a failed suicide attempt in the early hours of the morning.

The family of David Peterson – a previous lover of White who was killed by White in an act that was deemed self-defence 3-years ago – are calling for the police to look into the original case again in light of White's recent murder convictions. It seems her body count could well be higher than previously thought.

Detective inspector Broadbent - who was the officer who finally brought an end to her reign of terror declined to comment.

Printed in Poland
by Amazon Fulfillment
Poland Sp. z o.o., Wrocław